What Reviewers Say About Bold Strokes Books

"With its expected unexpected twists, vivid characters and healthy dose of humor, *Blind Curves* is a very fun read that will keep you guessing."—*Bay Windows*

"In a succinct film style narrative, with scenes that move, a character-driven plot, and crisp dialogue worthy of a screenplay…the Richfield and Rivers novels are…an engaging Hollywood mystery…series."—*Midwest Book Review*

Force of Nature "…is filled with nonstop, fast paced action. Tornadoes, raging fire blazes, heroic and daring rescues… Baldwin does a fine job of describing the fast-paced scenes and inspiring the reader to keep on turning the pages." —*L-word.com Literature*

In the Jude Devine mystery series the "…characters seem fully capable of walking away from the particulars of whodunit and engaging the reader in other aspects of their lives."—*Lambda Book Report*

Mine "…weaves a tale of yearning, love, lust, and conflict resolution…a believable plot, with strong characters in a charming setting."—*JustAboutWrite*

"While these two women struggle with their issues, there is some very, very hot sex. If you enjoy complex characters and passionate sex scenes, you'll love *Wild Abandon*."—*MegaScene*

"*Course of Action* is a romance…populated with a host of captivating and amiable characters. The glimpses into the lifestyles of the rich and beautiful people are rather like guilty pleasures…a most satisfying and entertaining reading experience."—*Midwest Book Review*

The Clinic is "…a spellbinding novel."—*JustAboutWrite*

"*Unexpected Sparks* lived up to its promise and was thoroughly enjoyable…Dartt did a lovely job at building the relationship between Kate and Nikki."—*Lambda Book Report*

"*Sequestered Hearts*…is everything a romance should be. It is teeming with longing, heartbreak, and of course, love. As pure romances go, it is one of the best in print today." —*L-word.com Literature*

"*The Exile and the Sorcerer* is a mesmerizing read, a tour-de-force packed with adventure, ordeals, complex twists and turns, and the internal introspection of appealing characters."—*Midwest Book Review*

The Spanish Pearl is "…both science fiction and romance in this adventurous tale…A most entertaining read, with a sequel already in the works. Hot, hot, hot!"—*Minnesota Literature*

"A deliciously sexy thriller…*Dark Valentine* is funny, scary, and very realistic. The story is tightly written and keeps the reader gripped to the exciting end."—*JustAbout Write*

"*Punk Like Me*…is different. It is engaging. It is life-affirming. Frankly, it is genius. This is a rare book in that it has a soul; one that is laid bare for all to see."—*JustAboutWrite*

"*Chance* is not a novel about the music industry; it is about a woman discovering herself as she muddles through all the trappings of fame."—*Midwest Book Review*

Sweet Creek "…is sublimely in tune with the times." —*Q-Syndicate*

"*Forever Found*...neatly combines hot sex scenes, humor, engaging characters, and an exciting story."—*MegaScene*

Shield of Justice is a "…well-plotted…lovely romance…I couldn't turn the pages fast enough!"—Ann Bannon, author of *The Beebo Brinker Chronicles*

The 100th Generation is "…filled with ancient myths, Egyptian gods and goddesses, legends, and, most wonderfully, it contains the lesbian equivalent of Indiana Jones living and working in modern Egypt."—*Just About Write*

Sword of the Guardian is "…a terrific adventure, coming of age story, a romance, and tale of courtly intrigue, attempted assassination, and gender confusion…a rollicking fun book and a must-read for those who enjoy courtly light fantasy in a medieval-seeming time."—*Midwest Book Review*

"*Of Drag Kings and the Wheel of Fate*'s lush rush of a romance incorporates reincarnation, a grounded transman and his peppy daughter, and the dark moods of a troubled witch—wonderful homage to Leslie Feinberg's classic gender-bending novel, *Stone Butch Blues*."—*Q-Syndicate*

Wall of Silence "…is perfectly plotted and has a very real voice and consistently accurate tone, which is not always the case with lesbian mysteries."—*Midwest Book Review*

In *Running with the Wind* "…the discussions of the nature of sex, love, power, and sexuality are insightful and represent a welcome voice from the view of late-20-something characters today."—*Midwest Book Review*

"Rich in character portrayal, *The Devil Inside* is an unusual, unpredictable, and thought-provoking love story that will have the reader questioning the definition of right and wrong long after she finishes the book."—*JustAboutWrite*

By the Author

I Dare You

No Leavin' Love

The Pleasure Planner

The Pleasure Planner

by

Larkin Rose

2009

THE PLEASURE PLANNER

ISBN 10: 1-60282-121-6
ISBN 13: 978-1-60282-121-7

This Trade Paperback Original Is Published By
Bold Strokes Books, Inc.
P.O. Box 249
Valley Falls, NY 12185

First Bold Strokes Printing: October 2009

Credits
Editor: Cindy Cresap
Production Design: Stacia Seaman
Cover Design By Sheri (graphicartist2020@hotmail.com)

Acknowledgments

To Cindy and Jennifer…Thank You!

Dedication

To my readers: You are the reason I keep my fingers flying across this keyboard.

Mira…for handing down the title.

Jove…for those late-night brainstorming sessions. You're awesome!

India…hurry up with school already! Miss ya and mean it, dammit!

Dalia…for your endless critiques and priceless friendship. I have no idea what I'd do without you. Love ya. Mwah!

To my children and grandbabies…you are my whole world.

To Rose…Uh-Huh!

Chapter One

Brianna Hendricks, professional lesbian matchmaker, wheeled her Lotus Elise into the drive leading up to the colonnaded entrance of the Golden Mirage, arguably the best hotel in all of San Francisco. The valet was there a heartbeat before she cut the engine and she took his hand as he assisted her out of the car.

"Thank you." She smiled politely.

"You are most welcome, miss." He accepted the generous tip and gave her a brief salute.

She paused and looked out over the bay while she adjusted her Bluetooth to receive an incoming call. "Bree Hendricks."

"Bree, this is Monica. I've got a problem. I think…I'm sure…I screwed up my date with Carla Summers, again. She stormed out of the restaurant, calling me every name but Buttercup. I swear I was only fifteen minutes late, and even phoned ahead to arrange for a bottle of Cristal to be chilling on our reserved table."

Bree mentally counted backward from ten, her spiked heels punctuating the countdown as she tip-tapped across the Italian marble floor of the portico toward the entrance. She'd been practicing this calming technique for months, and though it worked with some of her clients, she was beginning to lose her patience with this particular client. Monica was one of her more stubborn clients, resisting Bree's advice every step of the way. Through their meetings and meet-n-greets with possible clientele, she'd actually begun to consider Monica a friend, thank goodness, because right now she was on the verge of going postal on her.

She slipped her BlackBerry into the pocket of her white pinstriped Armani suit jacket. "Are you fucking kidding me? What in hell's name was Carla doing at the restaurant before you? Didn't you listen to anything I said during our consultation meeting? Never, *ever*, let your date arrive before you. Ever!"

"I know…I'm sorry, Bree. Something came up at the last second."

She took a calming breath and slipped her arm through the strap of her purse as she continued at a steady pace through the lobby. "Listen, Monica, you can't expect a woman of her stature to sit patiently, drumming her freshly manicured nails on the table, while you take your sweet friggin' time. Women like Carla want to make a grand entrance. They want to see the way your brow arches as your gaze sweeps down their body, the sparkle of desire in your eyes when you see their brand new designer dress, how well it snugs their curves. They want you to see their newly purchased spiked stilettos as they saunter your way as if they have nothing better to do. Do you understand me? They want all the attention focused on them, and they want that attention from you…you!"

"Yes, but—"

"No buts! You've placed your confidence in me, and paid me handsomely, I might add, so we're no longer playing by your rules. We're playing by *mine*. And if I'd been Carla, waiting all alone for you to get your lazy ass to my date, I'd have poured the ice bucket over your crew cut head and carried that damn bottle home with me."

Increasing her pace, Bree left the lobby. Her heels sank into the dark burgundy carpet as she moved swiftly down the corridor toward the luxuriously appointed ballroom. However, there was no need to rush. She was never late. Tardiness was her biggest pet peeve. The auction wasn't due to start for another thirty minutes. Besides, Bree didn't know how to be late to anything and no excuse would overcome punctuality. "Now, this is what I'm going to do for you. I'm going to call Carla and let her know you were a jackass, that you want to apologize for your unforgivably rude behavior in person over a candlelight dinner in the darkest corner of Kuleto's Italian restaurant, and see if I can drum you up yet another date. And if you screw this one up, I'm going to release you from your contract and wish you a good life. Am I making myself clear?"

"Bree, that's not fair."

"Fair? Sure it is. Your signature on the contract in my filing cabinet proves that point. Do you want the date or not? Or should I find Carla another woman who will make sure she's not left sitting alone, and who will stare at her with star-struck eyes when she sashays across the room? In short, somebody who will be seated and waiting with bated breath for her entrance."

Monica's exasperated sigh drifted down the line. "Yes. Yes, dammit, I want another date with her. She looked so edible in that slinky dress, not to mention those spiked heels with sexy ribbons climbing her legs…and when she stormed across the room I—"

"Uh-huh. You didn't forget about the little clause in your contract about no *sex*, did you?"

"Hell no. How could I forget about that? It's sadistic—like cutting off a man's dick."

Bree chuckled. As much as Monica raked her nerves sometimes, she was a great person and meant well. "Good. I'll set it up, but so help me God, if you fuck this one up, I'll castrate your brassy female balls with a rusty butter knife. Got it?"

Monica laughed. "Aye, aye, sir. I'll be on my best behavior and I'll arrive an hour before the date. Promise."

"You better. And make sure you have a single pink ranunculus. It's her favorite. And you better go on and on about how beautiful she is, and what a sorry sack of shit you were for being late."

"Anyone told you what a hard ass you are?"

Bree smiled as she spotted her personal assistant and only true friend, Sienne, tapping her red pump impatiently just inside the ballroom doors, arms crossed in that "I'm already pissed at you" posture. "Yep. I've been told that a time or two. But don't forget, I'm a hard ass for your best interest. I'm the one searching for your soul mate."

"For that, I thank you. Sorry I was late. I know you worked hard to pick out the best date for me."

"Damn right, I did. And don't tell *me* you're sorry, tell Carla. Gotta go. Kisses."

Bree disconnected the call and gave Sienne a toothy grin and a low whistle. She was used to seeing her in casual clothing, mainly jeans and T-shirts around the office. Tonight's outfit, however, oozed sophistication. Her long legs were encased in silvery gray slacks topped off with a red silk top that scooped low to reveal a deep cleavage. Her short brown hair was moussed into an array of waves, making her look way younger than her thirty-six years. "Wow. You resemble someone looking for a lay. I take it someone *special* will be here tonight?"

Sienne gave her a cocky grin. She was dressed up for a reason, and that reason was somewhere here in this building, probably handing out her own flyers for her travel agency. Sienne had been crushing on her for months. "Don't try to make nice with me. Why were you making business calls on your night off?" She reached for Bree's Bluetooth and gently pulled it from her ear. "You promised tonight was going to be a laid back night. I *only* gave you permission to hand out cards and possibly make an appointment or four." She pulled Bree's purse off her shoulder.

Bree arched her brow. "Since when does an assistant tell the boss what to do?"

"Since the boss works too damn hard and her assistant is the only damn friend she has to make sure she doesn't overwork herself. And don't change the subject. Who were you talking to?"

"It was Monica…our pain in the ass client for way too many months now. I swear she's trying to make my hair turn gray. She was late for her date with Carla, *again*." Bree reached for the earpiece but Sienne jerked backward then held out her hand.

"That's because she thinks it's all about her. Now give me the phone."

"I promise I won't make any more calls." Bree held her hand protectively over her pocket.

"I know you won't, as soon as you give it to me." Sienne nudged her hand forward, stern expression on her face. "Hand it over."

Bree rolled her eyes, withdrew the BlackBerry from her pocket, and handed it over. "You're a pushy little thing."

"Yeah, well, working alongside a hard ass all day tends to rub off on people. Now lose the jacket. And unbutton that blouse. You look like a schoolmarm."

Bree glanced down her body, taking in her silk rose pink blouse sealed against her curves. "You don't think this is sexy?"

Sienne closed the gap between them and plucked open two buttons, pulling the material apart. "Now it is. And when you take off the jacket everyone will see that fine ass of yours."

"Why, exactly, do I want everyone seeing my cleavage and ass?"

"Because you have a sexy body and tonight you need to unwind."

"And my body has what to do with having a drink and drumming up more business?"

Sienne let out a breath. "Jesus, just give me the fucking jacket."

Bree shrugged out of the jacket and handed it to Sienne. "Dammit, woman, you're getting bossier by the second."

"Thank you. I take that as a compliment coming from the queen bitch herself." Sienne winked then headed for the coat closet.

Bree moved further into the ballroom, a glittering symphony of green silk-covered walls and Bavarian crystal chandeliers that shot rainbows of color in all directions. Matching crystal wall sconces added sparkle to the luxuriously set tables. She looked toward the stage where the auction would take place. On the block were ten women who'd volunteered their services to help raise money for a local homeless shelter.

Women were everywhere in small and large groups, some already seated at the round tables draped with linen cloths, but most were standing idly by, waiting for the auction to begin. Dykes, femmes, butches, all dressed to the nines, anxious to see and be seen at one of the glitziest charity events on the social calendar.

Bree scanned the throng and easily identified outfits from at least twenty of the most influential designers. She gave a satisfied smile at the array of gorgeous choices for every available woman in the room. These occasions were also the perfect opportunity to hand out her business cards. And, with the overdose of hormones pumping strong through the crowd, she had an excellent chance to add real substance to her clientele list.

"Ms. Hendricks!" Someone called from behind her.

Bree turned to find a petite auburn haired woman with striking blue eyes framed by over-long fake lashes shoving her way through a small group of women. Costume diamonds sparkled against her earlobes and throat. Bree knew instantly this woman was a gold digger. She didn't question her natural instincts to read people. She just trusted them, and it helped tremendously when it came time to find matches for her clients.

This woman required lavish attention, so high-maintenance was a given while Bree took in her freshly French manicured nails with more bling on her fingers than should be allowed.

The woman came to a breathless halt in front of Bree, so close she invaded the invisible line of her personal territory. "I wanted to talk to you about your services."

Bree mentally flipped her Rolodex of clients looking for a suitable match for someone who needed extra special care. She thought of one name instantly—a millionaire looking for someone to coddle with her money and not ashamed to admit those desires. "Sure. Let me give you a card." Bree produced a business card. "Call the office tomorrow and my assistant can set you up an appointment for an interview."

The woman extended her hand and wiggled her fingers seductively as she slowly withdrew the paper from Bree's grasp. Bree bit back a smile as she watched the femme bat her lashes. "How long does it take you to find someone's true love? I hear your success rate is sky high."

Bree grinned. This woman wasn't looking for love. She was looking for a fat bank account from a sugar mama. "That depends on what you're looking for, and if we have available clients with those complementary requirements. If we don't, it's my job to go out and find what you're looking for."

The woman read the card. "'Love Match...*strike a flame that burns forever*.' How charming."

Bored with this simpering, Bree switched her attention to the rest of the room, taking in the few women already gathered on the stage. The announcer stood nearby watching the event staff adjusting the wires for the sound system and microphone.

Her gaze halted abruptly on two other women talking intently to each other at the side of the stage. Bree's heart stuttered as she studied one in particular, dressed in loose blue jeans, a gray tank top, and a sheer overshirt; she looked stunning in a casual kind of way. Her hair was feathered back on the sides, the top a mass of thick brown curls. She looked totally out of place against the prestigious crowd of sophisticated women, like she'd just wandered in from a long stroll on a windy beach without bothering with appearance afterward.

Bree assumed her to be with the set-up crew. And she couldn't stop staring, wondering what kind of woman would dress down for such an occasion, yet still stand out like a diamond.

The woman beside her cleared her throat and Bree suddenly remembered she'd been carrying on a conversation with a possible client. She turned back, an apologetic smile on her lips. "I'm sorry. I was looking for my assistant."

"No problem." The woman held out a card and Bree took it, casually glancing down at the name printed in hot pink cursive letters. "I'd really like to set up a meeting at your earliest convenience."

"Great. I'll have my assistant get in contact with you as soon as possible."

The woman nodded then sashayed away on pink stilettos. Bree immediately switched back to the women still chatting near the stage, letting her gaze travel down the length of the shorter one. She wanted to know her name…and, more importantly, what she'd sound like when an orgasm tore from her body.

Sienne came to stand beside Bree and nudged her with her shoulder. "Please, God, tell me you gave her a card. Helen would cream her panties over that one."

"Sure did. Here's her card." Bree held out the paper and Sienne plucked it from her grasp. "This one's a definite gold digger. Make sure you get her in early next week so I can make Helen a happy woman."

"No problem." Sienne grinned and they both turned back to the waiting crowd. "Now tomorrow, nine a.m. sharp, you have a meeting with Taylor—at Starbucks—about her date night before last. She said things went great. At ten, you have to meet Ms. Beechum around the corner at the sandwich shop. She's ready to choose from the new models. I've already set up your home visit with her as well, for next Tuesday."

Bree only half-listened to Sienne, her attention fixed on the woman across the room. She was smiling at the very tall woman beside her, but from the looks of their posture, they weren't together. What was it about her? She sure didn't resemble anything Bree normally found sexy. Hell, far from it. But there was something about her, something that screamed independent, strong-willed, and I don't give a shit what people think about me. Bree liked that in a woman.

As if sensing her interest, the woman turned and their eyes met. Something in that hypnotic stare held Bree rooted to her spot. She felt like the woman had somehow seen deep into her soul. The woman broke eye contact first, and her gaze lazily swept down Bree's body before she turned back to her friend.

"Excuse me. I'm trying to have my brief meeting with you so you don't get your clients mixed up tomorrow." Sienne waved her PDA in front of Bree's face.

"Like I've ever gotten my appointments mixed up." Bree struggled to get her breathing under control.

"Who the hell are you looking at?"

"No one. Just waiting for the auction to begin so I can build up my clientele." Bree turned away, trying to compose herself. She felt like a teenager lusting after her first piece of ass.

"Uh huh, right." Sienne turned to scan the crowd. "So who is it that's stolen your undivided attention?" She gasped. "Oh my God, there's Tawny. I have to go say hi." Flustered, Sienne pressed down her shirt. "Do I look okay?"

Bree gave her a reassuring smile. "You look fantastic. Go talk to her."

A hint of crimson swept across Sienne's cheeks. "I'll meet back up in a minute to continue our conversation."

As soon as the crowd swallowed Sienne, Bree darted to the coat closet, feeling awkwardly naked without her BlackBerry, and her pussy in need of much attention.

❖

"I can't believe I let you talk me into this shit." Logan watched a group of four chic bitches giggle and nudge each other, no doubt part of the idiot clique who'd volunteered their time to be auctioned off for a date. Hell, she was one of those idiots this year.

How she'd let Paula talk her into this nonsense she'd never know. She could be in her loft finishing up the body art for Elise Simon instead of feeling completely out of place among these rich, designer clad women. Truly, she felt like a black panther in the middle of a room of jaguars and leopards.

Except for the woman across the room who'd just parted the crowd like the Red Sea, there wasn't anyone here who quirked her brow. Where had she gone? Was the woman talking to her only minutes ago her date? Logan wanted to know. Had to know.

"I think you should go talk to her. You could damn well use her services." Paula stepped back as two more women barged toward the stage.

"Who?"

"Brianna Hendricks, the professional matchmaker you've been drooling over for the past fifteen minutes."

Logan turned to look up at Paula, all six foot one inches of her. Her dark eyes looked almost black against the dim lighting. "I was not drooling over her."

"Don't know why. She's fucking hot as hell."

Logan grinned. That was an understatement. The woman oozed dominance, her straight posture exuded arrogance. Logan normally avoided women like her, with their noses to the air. But that expression didn't translate to "I'm better than everyone around me" for this woman. It said "I'm confident with myself." Logan could live with that...and she wanted to fuck her so bad it made her head swim.

Someone stopped beside Paula and introduced herself. Logan barely heard the exchange of names, her feet were already in motion leading her across the room. She had to get close to that woman, if only for a minute, if only for one solid second. She needed to smell her.

Following the same route she was sure this Brianna had taken, Logan found herself outside the coatroom. She took a brief glance inside but didn't see anyone. When she turned to walk away, she heard mumbled female cursing and knew her mystery goddess was making the racket.

With a moan of animalistic instinct, she stepped inside the closet and found the object of her infatuation digging in the pockets of a coat.

"Dammit, where'd she put it?" Brianna jerked the coat around and dug in the opposite pockets.

"Are you picking pockets? Don't you know it's against the law?"

Brianna whipped around, her hands outstretched against the hanging coats. "Jesus! Don't sneak up on people like that." She held her hand to her heart.

Logan noticed immediately her fingers were well manicured, but lacked the stylish length she detested. A dark shade of maroon nail polish covered each nail, and there was no ring of possession on her left hand.

She took a step toward Brianna, watched in awe as those deep green eyes narrowed. "You didn't answer the question."

Brianna blinked and straightened. "My assistant is determined I'm not working tonight, and took my cell phone. I'm trying to find it."

"Mmm-hmm."

Brianna's lips parted and her tongue snaked out to caress the corner of her mouth.

Logan wasn't sure what possessed her, or what the hell overcame her in one second flat, but she found herself closing the gap, unable to stop herself.

Brianna didn't even flinch, and her expression invited Logan's kiss.

Logan hovered over her, her own breath heaving in her chest, though her nerves were abnormally calm to be acting so foolishly. "I'm going to kiss you, Brianna Hendricks, professional matchmaker."

"You think?" Brianna stared intently at Logan's lips and her hands fisted on both sides of her hips, gripping material of several coats.

"I know." Logan leaned down and barely pressed her lips against Brianna's. Her head swam for a brief second, her heart hammering in her chest. A sweet, intoxicating aroma met her nose and she inhaled, and then parted Brianna's lips with her tongue.

Brianna moaned, the sound like a gentle caress of wings against her cheek. Logan wanted to slam her body up against a wall, wanted to grab her legs and wrap them around her hips then grind against her until she expelled an orgasm.

Instead, she tasted her, melding their tongues in a duel of exploration while she reached down and pulled Brianna's tight grip away from the coats. She wove their fingers together and pressed her deeper against the coats.

"Bree, dammit, I knew I'd find…oh, shit, um…"

Logan pulled away from Brianna but didn't turn around. She watched her eyes lazily flutter open, her lips moist from their kiss.

With a groan, Brianna blinked and stepped to the side, staring at Logan like she'd never set eyes on her.

"Natalie called, she just landed, and, shit…said you're still on for tonight," the woman behind them said.

Logan wondered who Natalie was, then remembered the woman she was kissing was a matchmaker, and it seemed she was always in work mode. No wonder her assistant had stolen her cell phone.

Brianna took a deep breath, her eyes wide with trepidation. She swiped the back of her hand across her mouth. "Shit, I, uh…fuck. Okay, thanks, Sienne."

"I need all contestants to the stage at this time," the PA system announced.

Logan took a step back, still staring into those hypnotic eyes. "I have to go."

Brianna nodded, her chest rising and falling with staggered breaths. "Okay."

Logan leaned toward her, watched Brianna's eyes widen and her lips part as if she expected another kiss. "You taste delicious. I knew you would." She turned away, nodded to the assistant, and then darted from the closet.

Chapter Two

Bree came back to herself in a whirlwind of emotions. Feeling like an amnesia victim who'd suddenly awakened from a deep sleep, she remembered her name, her occupation, that she was thirty-four, and that she had a fucking girlfriend…Natalie Gerald, a prestigious lawyer working for one of the hottest law firms in San Francisco.

Fuck. What the hell was wrong with her?

She fell against the coats and let out a loud sigh. "Holy shit. What have I done? I have no idea what just came over me."

Sienne rushed to her side. "Sweet heavens, you're forgiven. She was hot as sin. I'd do her myself, single or not."

Bree chuckled and shook her head. "I can't believe I just kissed a total stranger in a fucking coat closet. For crying out loud, I have a girlfriend. What kind of cheating freak would do that?"

"A horny one? Who the hell cares? Besides, this is the biggest friggin' coat closet I've ever seen. You could set up a damn swimming pool in this bitch." Sienne angled her head. "Go bid on her, then take her home and fuck her all night. I'll make up some excuse to keep Natalie off your back."

Startled, Bree straightened. “Oh my God, she’s one of the contestants!” She pushed past Sienne and made her way into the crowded ballroom. Everyone had shoved their way toward the stage, eagerly anticipating the beginning of the auction.

The woman who no doubt had Bree’s pale pink lipstick still smudged against her lips was standing in the middle of the line of women at the rear of the stage. She looked directly at Bree as if pleading with her to bid the highest when it came her turn.

“You’re flippin’ out of your mind if you don’t bid on that tight piece of ass.” Sienne came to stand beside her, smiling like a demented fool.

“I’ll do no such thing.” But Jesus, how she wanted to fuck that woman, to have her thrust an orgasm out of her body…to satisfy the one eagerly demanding attention right now.

She squeezed her legs together to ease the ache while the announcer called out participant number one, giving her full name and a brief resume of her talents. Dressed in pumps, a slinky black dress that shouted Versace, her hair woven into a grotesque mass of curls resembling a beehive, the woman strutted across the stage to thunderous applause.

Not her type at all. Bree shook her head against the alien thoughts. Her type was in her car, headed home, while Bree stood gawking at a lineup of sexy women. No, one sexy woman in particular, the rest were nobodies. Her type was intelligent, cool, and sophisticated, and would be fucking her brains out within the next two hours. Her type had a name—Natalie.

They’d met at a private party just shy of a year ago, and though there were no flashing neon signs to advocate their connection, the sex had been incredible…and still was.

Things were normal, and routine, with Nat…just the way Bree liked life. They each had their own homes, their own lives, and when time allowed, they spent that free time with one another. Her mom called them boring. Bree considered them relaxed.

She forced Natalie's image out of her mind and focused on the stage. The bidding moved forward briskly until the first woman found a winning bidder and stepped off the stage, smiling sweetly at her waiting date.

With a moan of self-loathing at the vulgar thoughts rushing through her mind of all the things she wanted to do to her mystery kisser, Bree watched as the next woman walked across the stage. She wore flat gold strappy sandals and a retro outfit of a long, flowing brown hippie style skirt with a matching gypsy blouse, flirtatiously batting her glitter-laden eyelashes.

By the time the fourth participant stepped forward, the audience was packed tightly against the edge of the stage like groupies at a Grateful Dead concert. It was then that Bree realized they were anticipating the woman she'd kissed in the damn closet. Who could blame them? Even dressed down and completely out of place, she was sexy as sin, as Sienne had put it. She more than oozed sex appeal. Hell, she was a walking Venus flytrap. And Bree wanted to fuck her like she'd never wanted to fuck another woman.

It was sick, actually. Bree prided herself on her self-control. Right now, she had zilch. She wanted to let loose and just be…just be something she normally wasn't. And she wanted to do it with the sexy butch about to step into the limelight.

Bree moved closer, mentally cursing herself for even considering bidding. This was a night for building clientele, not searching for a quick fuck that she'd never see again. She wasn't into one-night stands, or cheating on her girlfriend. Rather, she never had been, but tonight her iron morals appeared to be a bit flexible. Not that she could truly call Natalie a girlfriend. They were more like sexual acquaintances who liked the routine of coming and going as they pleased. But right now, she was ready to toss her beliefs out the window to fuck this woman for one night…for one hour, for one fucking orgasm.

Woman number four stepped off the opposite side of the stage where her winner was waiting, and then Bree held her breath while the sexy kissing bandit moved forward.

"Here we have Logan Delaney. Thirty-five, single, and one of the finest artists San Francisco has ever seen. She specializes in nude body art, so, ladies, make sure you grab her business card before you head out those doors tonight."

Logan. Even the name sounded sexy, and Bree wanted nothing more than to feel the vibration of her name screaming from her lips.

The women surrounding the stage surged closer, jostling for the best position, their shrill cries and applause echoing around the vast ballroom. They bounced on their heels and craned their necks, pushing deeper into the mixture of dykes and femmes.

Sienne pushed Bree forward and added her voice to the hoots and catcalls of excitement. The bidding began at one thousand dollars. No doubt, the auctioneer knew starting beneath that number would be a waste of her time with the crowd already waving their hands in eager anticipation of winning a date.

Sienne grabbed Bree's hand and held it high above her head. The auctioneer acknowledged her bid then immediately did the same for another woman stabbing her hand in the air.

"Stop it!" Bree jerked her hand from Sienne's grasp.

"Oh, don't give me that shit. You know you were about to do it, just needed a little boost." A wicked grin broke across Sienne's face and then she winked. "Do it, girl. What do you have to lose?"

"Um, like a girlfriend?"

Sienne waved her hand in dismissal. "Yeah, whatever. If that's what you call a girlfriend then I need to start calling Rocky my boyfriend. He fetches my slippers and the newspaper every morning. That's more than I can say for Natalie."

God, it was true. Bree sighed. They barely had any coherent conversations that didn't consist of "your place or mine" and "how about dinner at so and so?" Had she somehow trapped herself into a relationship of content fucks where things always stayed the same, nothing ever out of the ordinary? Natalie never rang her for that last minute intimate chat between lovers when she was away on business. Hell, she couldn't remember when they'd last spoken, let alone had a proper conversation. And their sex life followed the same pattern. A quick explosive fuck then Nat retreating back to her own little world of client files leaving Bree to fend for herself as though she didn't exist for Natalie outside of the bedroom.

Bree looked back at the stage. She licked her lips as Logan slowly unbuttoned her shirt, spurred on by the crowd's cheers. Fuck, could the woman get any sexier? Bree chewed the inside of her cheek as Logan dropped the shirt off her shoulders. Of course she had to have cut muscles lining those tanned arms, and that dimple was making the women lose their fucking minds as she smiled down over them.

The bidding grew to three thousand within minutes and Bree couldn't help herself...she raised her hand.

Sienne cheered and whistled through her fingers.

Logan winked at Bree.

Bree's insides turned to mush and her pussy throbbed intently for relief.

At five thousand, Bree was out of her mind with a need she'd never encountered before. She had to have this woman, tonight, right now, back in that damn closet, or anywhere.

Sienne nudged her. "You are so going to get fucked hard tonight."

Bree gasped and stepped back. What in the hell did she think she was doing? This was not the way professionals were supposed to act. She was a matchmaker, for crying out loud. Half the people in this room knew her, knew of her business. What in hell's name could they possibly think of her right now? All in the name of charity? Yes. Dammit, that's what it was.

Fuck! No, it wasn't. This had nothing to do with charity, or those poor homeless kids. She took one last glance at the woman she wanted to tear apart with her bare teeth, then turned and rushed back through an almost empty room behind her. Needing to distance herself from temptation, she practically dove against the drink bar and pointed to the first wine bottle she saw.

As soon as the bartender handed her the glass, she downed it, needing her mind empty, her thoughts gone. Fire scorched her throat and she coughed while giving the bartender a glare wondering what in the world she'd just drank.

The crowd cheered, drawing her sights back to the stage, to Logan working the crowd like a magician. Jesus, she'd just about won a date with a complete stranger and was yearning to do all the sinfully yummy images dancing through her mind…the same things she demanded her clients never do.

She would have fucked that woman until the break of dawn. And from the look of those eyes, devouring her from atop the stage, it would have been a damn good fuck.

❖

Logan twirled her date around the dance floor. Slender, standing maybe five foot two inches even on spiked heels, the woman wasn't anywhere near her idea of sexy. Sure, she liked a goddess prowling toward her in sexy shoes, one eagerly willing to be her one-night stand, but she liked her women just a little taller, the ones who fit perfectly right beneath her chin.

Not that it truly mattered. She wasn't with a woman long enough to see where she fit, be it under her chin, in the crook of her arm, and especially not holding her hand. Sweet nothings didn't figure into her personal dictionary when she was fucking her quickies—usually her married, straight clients who posed no threat to her secluded lifestyle. Although Brianna, she imagined, would feel perfect rocking beneath her weight.

She shook her head to swipe away the thoughts. The woman had made it clear that kiss wouldn't go any further by halting her bids. Why hadn't she continued? Did she already have a lover, or a girlfriend? If that were the case, she'd proved herself unworthy of consideration. Logan held those who cheated on their partner in utter contempt. She sighed. Surely Brianna didn't fall into that category, mainly because she didn't want to give up on her yet.

Logan smiled as her date wedged herself against her, batting those way too thick lashes and craning her head back to look up at her with shit brown eyes.

God, how she wished she was twirling Brianna around

this floor, continuing what she desperately wanted to finish. And from the feel of her giving in to that kiss, the matchmaker wanted the same thing. There had to be a way to make it happen.

"Would you be so kind as to get me a drink? It's getting way hot in here." The woman, who Logan now knew was Stacy since she'd told her a few dozen times—along with her phone number—slicked her tongue along her bottom lip.

"You bet. I'll be right back." Logan practically ran from her, anything to get the hell away from the clingy woman. Only one more hour and she could get back to her paintings, back to her solitary life, just the way she liked it. Her studio loft was a godsend and when she couldn't sleep, with so many images weaving through her mind, she'd make her way down to the first floor to tinker with the old presses.

She was so close to figuring out how to make the dots and numbers into letters. Her agent, and especially Paula, swore it couldn't be done. Logan was determined to prove them wrong. Though, for what, she didn't know. What would the world make of a compilation of her grandfather's legendary articles melded into the famous photographs her grandmother had taken?

Probably nothing. But it was her dream and her striving need, and dammit, she was going to figure it out, and when she was done, maybe then she could breathe a sigh of relief that she'd honored their work. She almost hung her head in shame. Truth was, she'd already practically abandoned the idea, barely visiting the first floor anymore. Hell, she couldn't remember the last time she'd tinkered with the machines. Her clients, and her own sexual cravings, had come first for a very long time. Was she selfish, or just being practical?

Dismissing the questions, Logan cut through a group of giggling women at the bar and spotted Brianna with two women. *Brianna*—her heart skipped several beats. She moved closer, wanting to see her face one more time, to see her smile, to see those penetrating eyes.

When Brianna looked up and tagged her, Logan lost herself in those soft jade eyes. Long and lingering, Brianna continued her stare, telling her with those eyes alone how much she wanted Logan.

The bartender cleared his throat. Logan turned to look at him and rattled off her order. "Two vodka martinis, please."

When he set the drinks down, Logan could barely pull away from Brianna's smiling face long enough to retrieve the glasses.

She turned back toward the adjacent room, but something pulled her away and she found herself walking directly toward Brianna.

"The interviews are in three-part sessions…first in my office to get to know a little more about you, second being in your home, which seals my intuitions about the way you live, then finally a lunch date to go over available clients that I conclude fit for what you're looking for. And I must warn you, I don't leave any stone unturned. I take pride in my profession and I don't think you'd want anything less of me." Brianna briefly glanced at Logan then back to the woman. "I look forward to chatting again. My assistant will call you in the morning to go over fees and get your appointment set up."

"Thank you so much. I can't wait." The woman moved away, dragging her friend in her wake.

Brianna slowly turned to Logan and eyed the drinks in her hand. "For me? Why, thank you, ma'am." She winked and took one of the glasses. "Tell your date she'll have to fetch her own."

Logan laughed, loving Brianna's brashness…wanting

so bad to drag her back to that oversized closet and delve her fingers palm deep inside her. What was it about this woman that had her churning like a tropical storm from the inside out? "She can have mine."

"Aren't you the gentleman?" Brianna took a slow sip of her drink.

"I'm not gentle at all, if you'd like to discover, if you wanted." Logan wanted nothing more than to drop to her knees and rip those slacks off with her teeth, tear at Bree until she screamed out her name. Her heart was thrumming against her ears, her mind whirling with those very images.

Brianna's brow arched. "Your date is about ten steps behind you, like a Tasmanian devil in pursuit of her prey."

Logan wanted to growl as the woman's voice shrilled from behind her. "There you are. I thought you'd run off and left me all alone. Ah, my drink." She plucked the glass from Logan's grasp and gave Brianna a "back off because it's mine" glare.

Brianna barely acknowledged the woman with a quick look in her direction then back to Logan. "Don't forget to have your friend call tomorrow. I'm more than sure we can find just what she's looking for…in no time at all." Brianna held out her card and Logan found the strength to reach out and take it.

Lord help her, she was falling apart right before this gorgeous woman's eyes. "I'll have her call first thing in the morning. She'll be thrilled to have you at her service."

"I'll be more than happy to…assist her." Brianna took another sip of her drink, her sultry gaze meeting Logan's over the rim of her glass.

Logan's date pulled at her shirt. "Come on, sexy. You promised me another dance before our time ends." She tugged Logan harder, trying to pull her toward the dance floor.

Before her date could drag her too far, Logan withdrew one of her own cards from her jean pocket, cupped it in her palm, and extended her hand toward Brianna. "It was great to meet you, Brianna."

Brianna reached for her hand and shivers trailed up Logan's arm on contact. "Likewise, and please call me Bree." She shook her hand and took the card, then gave Logan a devilish smile as she read the contents. She winked and Logan shattered, her body ferociously hungry and aching.

Logan knew from the second she turned away, what they'd started was far from over.

Chapter Three

Bree pulled into the visitor parking slot outside Natalie's high-rise condo. She was a miserable horny mess desperate for relief. With a hurried flick of her wrist, she swiped her security card on the main door and stumbled across the lobby and into the elevator. In her eagerness to reach her goal, she practically clawed at the elevator door as it dragged open on the fourteenth floor.

Natalie's apartment stood at the far end of the interminably long hall. Bree staggered forward toward her door like a drunk on a mission, although she was perfectly sober, inserted the key she and Natalie had only swapped two months earlier, and unlocked the door.

After tossing her purse on the telephone stand by the door, she went in search of Natalie and found her curled up in the oversized chair with case files spread out across her lap. She barely even glanced up when Bree burst into the room. Typical Natalie. Bree shook her head; she'd done little more than shed her suit jacket before immersing herself in work. And how the hell did she manage to always look so good? Her makeup intact and her dark hair perfectly feathered back even after a five hour flight, and those sporadic auburn highlights she'd gotten last month showed up really well in the light from the desk lamp.

"You have three point two seconds to get that shit out of your lap before I pounce on you." Bree started working the buttons open on her blouse while Natalie arched a brow at her, surprise evident on her face.

Nat looked so sexy when she gave Bree that "holy shit, woman" expression. Bree wondered why she hadn't adopted a take-charge attitude more often, or anything that stripped away Nat's prissy veneer and left her with this delicious breathless look. She knew why...because that look wasn't one of sexual arousal; it was one of "you're stepping out of line" or "I'm too busy for these sex games."

Dismissing the thoughts, Bree stalked seductively toward her, slipping out of her blouse and dropping it onto the plush tan carpet. With barely a break in her stride, she yanked down her slacks and kicked out of them.

She closed in on Natalie, who sat immobile, like a frozen tableau with her glass of wine poised close to her pert lips. "These can go first." Bree snatched at the papers, placed them back into the folder, and tossed it onto the matching couch. She removed the wineglass from Nat's fingers and dropped into her lap, straddling her narrow thighs.

Natalie came slowly out of her trance and gripped Bree's hips, dragging her closer like a comforter. "I had a miserable flight, and an even more miserable meeting with those dickwads in New York. You have no idea what they—"

Bree leaned forward and silenced her with a kiss. She wasn't in the mood for conversation. Especially if, as usual, it focused upon Natalie's career, her cases, her files, her clients...rarely ever did they discuss Bree's life or her instinct for finding love for her own clients. Natalie didn't believe one could arrange a love match. She dismissed

Bree's arguments with scathing comments like "no amount of tinkering by anyone, other than the two parties involved, ever made a relationship bloom into love." Bree knew better. In today's world, people were too busy, too consumed by their occupations to open their eyes to the possibilities of love all around them. Her job was to help those people, and she did just that.

But tonight, she didn't want to talk about Natalie, or even herself. She just wanted to wipe Logan Delaney and that kiss clean from her mind with a good solid fuck, a powerful orgasm violently snatched from her body, until she quivered and shook with every harsh spasm.

She grabbed Natalie's hand and shoved it between her thighs, grinding it against her pussy in rough circles. "Feel how wet I am? I need you to fuck me, Natalie."

Natalie's eyes widened, no doubt disturbed by Bree's take charge behavior. In all their time together she'd played by Nat's unspoken rules and never initiated the action. By Natalie's choice, their sex was always robotic, always in bed, and always with Bree the pillow queen. Normally, she didn't mind—hadn't minded 'til now. Natalie was a great lover. She worked incredible magic with those experienced hands and always drew exquisite sounds of completion from Bree. Again, she wondered what kept her from taking the dominant role with Natalie.

"Dayum, baby! If I didn't know better, I'd think you actually had time to miss me." Natalie grinned, her even teeth bright against the light. "But not here..." Bree felt a shudder run through Natalie's body. "Let's take this to the bedroom."

"No. We do it right here. Right now." Bree scrabbled at Natalie's V-neck blouse and pulled her forward. She worked the material over her head then dove for her breasts, pulling the material of her bra down to expose a rosy nipple. Sucking, licking, and swirling her tongue over hardening nipples, all the while imagining how Logan's nipples would feel puckered against her lips, what she'd taste like.

In desperation to swipe Logan's face from her mind, she focused on the task, working Nat's nipple between her lips. Natalie placed her hands against Bree's waist and tried to push out of the chair, but Bree wouldn't budge. She grabbed Nat's hands and shoved them against the cushion of the chair on either side of her face. With Natalie's quizzical stare, Bree knew she was pushing the limits.

"What's got into you?" Natalie attempted a smile, but her eyes told a different story—she clearly didn't like Bree taking control.

Bree knew she should feel guilty for using Natalie, but she was beyond caring anymore. She needed release, and she needed it now. She struggled to get Logan's piercing eyes out of her mind while she bucked against Natalie. But Logan's steamy, strange kiss had been haunting her from the second she walked out of the coatroom.

God, what was wrong with her? Here she had a sexy woman, willing to satisfy her, and all she could think about was Logan's strong arms and that tight fucking ass. She should hate herself, she knew, but damn if the soaked mess between her legs didn't need satisfaction.

She closed her eyes and gave in to the images, grinding slowly with every flash of new pictures. Natalie leaned forward and licked the tip of Bree's nipple, gently sucking the hard bud into her mouth. Bree moaned and wanted to beg her to suck harder, faster, to finger fuck her, to keep plunging until Bree screamed out her release. She knew Natalie wouldn't oblige her needs. It would be a waste of time to plead for such uncharacteristic things.

When Natalie released the nipple, Bree came apart with impatience. She arched away from her and pumped against Natalie's pelvic bone. "Oh God, yeah. I need to come, Natalie."

To Bree's shock, Natalie worked one hand free and wiggled it between Bree's thighs. Bree held her breath, still arching and rounding her hips, and waited for penetration.

It didn't come. Natalie slid her thong aside and teased her pussy with the tip of one finger, slicking it through her juices and lightly flicking her clit. Bree slung her head back and pumped her hips, so close, so fucking close.

"Fuck me, Natalie. Please!" Bree thrashed, pumping and rolling her hips, sucking in healthy gulps of air, and all the while pictures of Logan played through her mind, touching her, caressing her, tasting her.

Sweet Jesus, she wanted to reach out and touch that virtual reality, wanted to fuck her so hard. Her insides burned like the pits of hell as Logan's image finger fucked her, controlling her orgasm, keeping her teetering on the edge of the abyss. She needed relief now or she was going to burn alive within minutes.

When Natalie teased her slit once again, Bree growled and reached between her legs. She grabbed Natalie's hand and shoved it deeper and then wiggled until thosc stiff fingers plunged inside of her.

"Make me come, dammit!" Bree cried out and rode Natalie, beyond caring that she was using Nat's body for her own satisfaction. When Natalie leaned forward and tentatively sucked Bree's nipple into her mouth, Bree wove her fingers into the strands of her hair and pulled Nat closer, encouraging her to take the breast deeper into her mouth. Natalie obeyed. She sucked harder, twisting the nipple between her teeth.

Bree bucked faster, riding those fingers, tugging her hair, and then her orgasm shattered. She thrashed against Natalie, slamming her pussy over those fingers buried deep inside, her voice hoarse as she screamed out her relief.

When her spasms eased and her muscles calmed to fluttering light pulses, Bree fell over Natalie, her insides twitching, her body spent…her mind twisting with torn emotions. This post orgasm moment should be about her and Nat and their closeness. Instead, Logan lingered in the depths of her thoughts.

Unsure of what to say, and definitely unsure of what to do, Bree just lay there, feeling like a total jerk for letting Natalie put out the fire Logan created. How sick of her… how shameful and utterly despicable.

"Feel better now?" Natalie chuckled, but the undertone screamed she wasn't happy about sex being out of routine.

Bree leaned backward, her hair escaped from their pins to spiral around her shoulders. "What'd you expect? You were gone four whole days." She pushed out of Natalie's lap and slid down to the floor.

She shoved Natalie's legs open and gave her a sexy smile, her fingers gliding up Nat's thighs toward her crotch. "Didn't you miss me, too?"

Natalie leaned down and kissed Bree on the forehead. "Of course I did, gorgeous." She pulled Bree back into her lap. "How about you grab us some snacks while I finish with this file?"

Bree blinked hard and angled her head. Somehow, she was seeing Natalie in a completely different light, and she didn't like what she saw. How could Natalie switch off like that? Hadn't her orgasm affected Nat, made her horny? Bree frowned. Was Natalie so wrapped up in her own sterile world that nothing, not even the promise of a raging orgasm at the hands and tongue of her lover, stirred her anymore? Content. That's what they'd become. Just two people playing sex games when time allowed, eager to have each other as arm candy.

How had she fallen into such a trap? Where was the love? Where was the tearing at each other because they'd missed their time together?

Those emotions were practically non-existent between them.

Bree kissed her on the cheek and pushed out of her lap. "Sure."

She dressed and made her way to the kitchen and gathered crackers, olives, and some cubed feta cheese that she knew Natalie loved to munch while agonizing over her case files, and then carried them all on a platter back to the living room.

Natalie was already deep in concentration, her brow furrowed as she flipped a page.

"I'm heading home." Bree set the tray on the coffee table. "Dinner tomorrow since I have back to back meetings the rest of the week?"

Natalie nodded and reached for a cracker. "You bet. Give me a call."

Bree studied her for several seconds before she left the apartment.

Convenient, that's what they were. Worse, though, was the sad fact it'd taken her so long to realize it. Worse still, she knew Natalie knew it too.

Chapter Four

Soft moonlight filtered through the open wide blinds to bathe Bree's bedroom in dull shadows. She awoke slowly, her mind still occupied with unanswered questions and images she desperately wanted out of her mind. As she stretched, the thin Egyptian sheets caressed her body like a lover's kiss, and she pondered why she couldn't relinquish the erotic thoughts of Logan, or why they'd kept her awake 'til the small hours. It wasn't the first time a sexy woman had kissed her.

But something was different with Logan. What was it about this one in particular who'd robbed her mind for so long—especially when she was a claimed woman?

She almost laughed at the thought. Who was she kidding? Natalie wasn't the claiming type. A good fuck, for sure, and a reliable one at that, but not a claimer.

Determined to find out why Logan had made such an impression, she shut off the alarm that had yet to buzz, then padded out to the kitchen. The house was quiet, always so quiet. She prided herself in the luxuries her job afforded her. Every room a showcase, decorated in the latest trends and fashions like an image ripped straight out of a glossy magazine, not a single item out of place. Hell, she was never home long enough to disturb anything except her four-poster bed, complete with ivory satin drapes.

Bree gave a quick snort at the crystal jar of lemons sitting on the long counter dividing the kitchen in half. They were for decoration only, adding cheery brightness to the otherwise bland white walls and countertops. She never had time to cook and Natalie preferred five-star restaurants as opposed to quiet dinners curled up on a couch. That is, when they had time. Besides, Natalie was a see and be seen kind of woman.

After pouring a mug of coffee, she carried it to the picture windows overlooking the bay. She loved this view, especially in the magical light of early morning, and today was no exception. A spiral of mist drifted across the water and wound itself through the bridge like a silken ribbon then dissipated all within a few minutes. Lights blinked on in the house across the street. Bree sighed and sipped her coffee. Time for her unknown neighbors to rise and shine, grab a shower and a quick breakfast, then drive off in pricy cars to their high-rise offices that earned the dollars to maintain their luxurious lifestyles.

She often wondered what they thought of her, the lone woman opposite, who was rarely at home, and who seldom had visitors. Did they wonder about her, watch her come and go, ever think about inviting her over for cocktails or Sunday brunch? Did it matter? Her life was already full enough not to need any more distractions. Though sometimes a little distraction was what she yearned for, something to knock her off the normalcy of her life.

With a shrug, she strolled into the living room to admire her collection of artwork dominating every available wall.

From bright abstracts by Jackson Pollock to autographed black-and-white celebrity photographs captured by some of the most famous photographers, she treasured each and every one.

After another sip of coffee, she spotted her purse lying on the loveseat where she'd tossed it last night. She walked over and dug inside, searching the evidence that Logan existed…that she'd really kissed her, that she'd wanted her with a vengeance.

She slowly withdrew the rectangular proof. Logan's business card claimed nude body art. What, exactly, did that mean? Bree frowned. Why had she never heard of her? Did Logan obtain her clients through word of mouth only? Most likely, she did. Bree imagined that type of artwork would require a very special relationship between artist and client.

Bree wanted to know a lot more about the woman who'd stolen her breath and disturbed her equilibrium with a brief kiss…to find out what made her different from all the others. There was only one way to get the answers—confront her tormentor. With an affirmative nod, she spun on her heels and made for her wet room. After a brief stint with the hair dryer and a few minutes applying makeup, Bree dressed in her favorite Armani suit, a midnight blue jacket and slacks teamed with matching silver and blue voile appliquéd blouse. She grabbed her laptop bag and purse then headed downstairs to the garage. Her hands trembled while she started the car and hit the button to open the doors. It wasn't like her to get edgy, or allow a woman like Logan to make her wander off her one-track mind of clients and finding love for each of them.

She took a deep breath to steady her nerves and then programmed the address in the GPS system before she maneuvered out of the driveway. By the time she pulled onto the commercial street, Bree was in a fever of anxiety and giddy with excitement, very much out of her character. With every strum of her heart, she was more determined to get answers and relieve the knotted mess churning in her stomach.

When she caught sight of the three-story red brick building, her mouth sagged open. She recognized it immediately. The first floor once housed one of the greatest magazine businesses Bree had ever had the pleasure of reading. *Malcolm and Adeline, The Real Life.* Of course, every article was from the past as they'd been shut down for well over ten years after the plane crash that took their lives, but Bree still cherished every one, adored how Adeline had captured the inner beauty of every person Malcolm interviewed. They were like the dynamic duo, writing articles about the rich and famous, not their public glamorous lives... but their inner lives, their secrets and dreams, their *real lives*. No other magazine had ever cared about the *real lives* of the faces behind the camera like those two had.

What a shame the new owners had turned it into a smutty, muckraking rag, and no surprise that this change had bankrupted it within three years. The business had never been reopened.

Bree parked against the curb and slowly made her way to the front door. Could those old printing presses still be there? Surely not. Whoever had purchased the building would definitely have had everything removed, and probably made a mint with the sale.

Unable to resist the urge, she stood on tiptoe and attempted to peek through the windows, but one of the large panes had been blackened with paint. She gave a disappointed sigh. What she wouldn't give to get her hands on more originals to match the one she'd purchased at an art auction several years ago.

Bree turned her attention back to the door and scanned the call buttons lining the edge, but none bore any names. She had no idea which floor Logan was on so she pressed the intercom for the first floor and waited. When the door didn't buzz, she pressed for the second floor—still nothing.

Aggravated, she jiggled the knob and smiled when the door opened. She stepped into a foyer of black and white tiles with a wide mahogany staircase to one side. She was tempted to knock on the only door…just to take a peek inside the world of the greatest minds she'd ever known, even though she'd never met them in person. Several walls in her house were adorned by the photocopies of her favorite articles.

Music started from one of the floors above her and she called out. "Hello?"

When no one answered, she started up the staircase. The sultry jazz mix grew louder as she climbed past the single closed door on the second floor and on up to the third. When she reached the top, she found the door open, the music now very loud.

She called out again and knocked on the doorframe. "Anyone here?" Giggling came from inside the room, so she stepped closer. "Logan?"

"Would you hold still? You're going to smear the paint." An exasperated sigh wove its way over the steady strum of chords. "Patience, my dear, patience."

Bree recognized that deep voice and her pussy throbbed.

Fuck! What was she doing here, at Logan's, with her

girlfriend hard at work right now? To get answers. Yes, that was it. Yeah right, who was she kidding? She'd come here to get fucked.

A female laughed. "Then hurry already. I can't wait much longer."

Bree stepped through the door to see a woman painted every color of the spectrum…Logan's face masked in a sensual smile as she stared up at the woman from her kneeling position on the floor, a paintbrush poised in her hand.

Bree gasped. It wasn't just any female. That was the one and only, Golden Globe award winner, Penny Carrow, best actress for the past three years, and very married. Didn't she have like two, maybe three, kids and a husband who was some kind of financial guru?

What the fuck was Logan doing with a woman like her? A sick coil formed in Bree's gut as she realized she'd almost walked in on Logan and Penny fucking. What kind of kinky shit was this bitch into? And what the hell was she going to do with that damn brush?

A flutter ripped through her stomach. "Shit, sorry. I was, just, um, looking for…" Bree took a step back, completely embarrassed and hating herself for needing answers. And for needing sex with the kissing bandit.

Logan froze…on her knees in front of her very married, and closeted bisexual, client, with her face inches from Penny's pussy.

The music was so fucking loud, but that glare Bree was shooting her was deafening. Her chest was heaving, her beautiful face flustered, her cheeks pink with embarrassment.

Dammit! She'd left the downstairs door unlocked after Penny had arrived. How could she be so stupid? Her clients deserved privacy, and they counted on Logan to keep their secrets just that, secret.

Penny turned away, hiding her face from Bree who, by that shocked expression, had already recognized her. Was that disgust glimmering in those striking green eyes? Who could blame her? Logan knew exactly what she was seeing, exactly what it looked like. Had Bree been ten minutes later, she'd have actually caught them fucking, every array of the rainbow merged against their bodies.

"So sorry. I'm in the wrong building." Bree turned and fled.

Logan could only stare at the empty doorframe. Her body screamed to chase her, to explain. But what was there to explain? The truth? How sick would that make her? The truth spelled out "paid whore to the closeted, rich and famous bisexuals," even if that sex came after the artwork.

Penny shifted. "Who the hell was that? Do you think she recognized me?"

Logan shrugged. "I don't think so. But I'll take care of it." She smiled at Penny. "Don't you worry your pretty little head about anything."

Penny reached for Logan.

Logan stood and kept her at arm's reach, not wanting to disturb the swirl of slow-drying colors painted on her client. God forbid she'd have to start all over, or have Penny's ritzy friends point out some minute flaw.

She knew the world Penny lived in, heard about it through the grapevine of friends that trailed behind Penny, all wanting their bodies captured in the same fashion. With her thoughts a jumbled mess, she ushered Penny toward the large canvas lying in the middle of her studio floor, already positioned over the oversized sheets, though her mind was still fixed on Bree…and that expression.

"You know the drill, sexy." Logan almost cringed with her words. She was flirting. She was always flirting. And always fucking—always fucking the married, closeted clients. How had she confined herself into this life? Not for the money, or the fame, nor the sex if truth be told. Although the money she earned would soon help finance the dream to honor her grandparents' life and work. And to a certain extent, she enjoyed the art side—the planning and execution of body art required skill, precision, and an eye for detail that was her forte.

These women didn't see anything in her except a means to captivate and woo their high-class friends. Logan gave them just that, with a bonus of sexual satisfaction while she protected their shameful secret.

Did that make her a monster? The world could never know the rich and famous had just been in her bed before they drove back to their normal, straight lives. And anyway, wasn't she free to fuck anyone she pleased?

Of course she was. But with Bree's glare still haunting her mind, she felt dirty and cheap, and wanted this session over as quickly as possible.

Penny knelt on the corner of the canvas. "This one will be mounted in my great room. I want everyone to be awed by my new body at my next party." She arched her back and glanced up at Logan. "And your talent, of course."

Logan swallowed a growl and picked up the remote control, then hit the button to lower the chain-suspended handles until they hovered over Penny's head. The models sometimes needed to move from one position to another, and being covered in paint made that a difficult task. The cloth-covered handles made it easier for them to adjust their bodies.

"Oooh. Those things are so kinky." Penny batted her lashes. "I think you should fuck me while I hang from them. You could tie me up and have your way with me before I go back to my drag of a life." She gave a sultry wink.

"That's an image worth investigating." Logan grinned and lowered herself to the floor, trying to ignore the fact that Penny's life was far from a drag. Few would refuse her fame, plus a lavish lifestyle with more money than she could spend on designer clothes and cosmetic surgery to enhance her image, and a nanny to babysit her children while she frolicked naked in Logan's studio, and only God knew what else she did, and with whom. Logan pushed back her thoughts to concentrate. "Now, slowly lay out in the center. Keep your hands against the outer edges in case I need you to move."

Penny did as instructed with Logan watching as her painted flesh made contact against the bright white board. She had only to push Penny's shoulder back once while her nipples pressed against the canvas.

"Perfect. Perfect!" Logan crawled to each side, making sure the paints hadn't squeezed out from under Penny, then pressed the button to lower the handles further. "Grab the handle and let me pull you up."

Penny reached for the bar and allowed the chains to lift her until she was standing on the edge, looking down over her own body captured in a spectrum of colors. Logan would only have to finish the edges with an array of abstracts, wait forty-eight hours for drying before adding several coats of acrylic. After that, she needed only to frame it, package it, and have it delivered.

She smiled at the work, happy with the choice of colors for this particular piece, then glanced up and found Penny's eyes dancing with desire.

Logan swallowed. Suddenly, she didn't want to fuck her client. She didn't want to be her secret release, the one Penny turned to when her itch needed scratching and hubby was too busy with his own career to worry about such needs.

Dammit, she wanted Bree to come back…wanted to fuck Bree with the same vengeance she fucked her clients.

She knew there was no hope for that. Bree's eyes told her what scum she was, that whatever could have been would never be. It strained her heart for some damn reason. Hell, she barely knew the beauty, but Lord help her, she wanted to know so much more about her.

When the phone rang, Logan practically dove for it.

"You done painting, or rather, fucking, your secret client?" Paula teased.

"Oh my God! When? Where?" Logan raked her fingers through her hair and faked despair.

"Um, here, and now? What the hell are you talking about?"

Logan had to turn her back to Penny to hide her smile. "Don't you move an inch. I'll be right there!" She hung up the phone and reached for her keys. "Penny, I've got to go. My friend needs my help. Can you please lock up after you shower?"

Logan went to her and took her hand. She placed a delicate kiss in the palm. "I'm so sorry I have to run out on you, especially with all those kinky images in my mind of you, dangling from those chains."

Penny smiled. "I'm demanding a rain check."

"You're on." Logan winked and flew from the studio, wanting to kick herself for giving up a free piece of ass—one who'd already paid her handsomely for her services, for her artwork, not the fuck.

Not that Bree would see that. But dammit, she had to try. Somehow, she had to make Bree understand that what she saw was not…

Fuck. Yes, it was.

Logan's heart plummeted as she descended the stairs two at a time.

CHAPTER FIVE

So, I'd like her age to be somewhere between twenty-five and twenty-nine," Addy announced, jarring Bree out of the fogged haze that had dogged her for an hour now.

She rocked back and forth in her desk chair, trying with every ounce of her being to focus on the prospective new client sitting across the desk from her.

What the hell was wrong with her? Why couldn't she concentrate on a simple task like listening? It was the essence of her job, listening to her clients. These meetings, home visits, and questionnaires were vital steps in her quest to form a rounded picture of her client's requirements and lifestyle. The whole process enabled her to link up the tiny, seemingly unimportant, morsels of information that normally sparked a perfect match. If one link in this chain broke or she missed a pivotal clue then the resulting match might end in disaster for both her client and ultimately her own business. The success of her business depended heavily upon satisfied clients who brought in more clients by word of mouth. Adverse comments could, in turn, bring the whole enterprise tumbling down around her ears.

It was all Logan's fault! The bitch!

Bree sighed. She hadn't been able to erase the barely glimpsed images before she fled Logan's studio. The artwork looked amazing, and from what little she'd seen, Logan had real talent, but the actress standing before Logan hadn't been art. Bree shuddered with the memory of Logan's face in close proximity to Mrs. Carrow's crotch. Only God knew what she was about to do with that damn brush.

Bree had tried to reason with herself that an artist would indeed need a brush to do the type of work Logan obviously did, but for some reason, she knew this time, it wouldn't have been used for that purpose.

It was sick, that's what it was. And she'd been embarrassed beyond description.

Bree couldn't help but wonder exactly how many more of Logan's so-called models were famous people who closeted their need for same sex satisfaction without the public stress. And Logan… Accepting payment for nude body art with "extras" was nothing short of whoring. Where was Logan's sense of decency, of right and wrong? And by the same token, Bree couldn't believe how she could find any woman who hired her body out for money attractive. Yet she did, and she was consumed by her own need to get close to Logan, to kiss her, touch her, taste her, and to fuck her until they were both sated. Logan had bewitched her with a single kiss. Entangled her in a web of deceit from which she couldn't escape. Every time she thought of kissing or touching Logan, she was in effect cheating on Natalie who, even if she gave little of herself in return, deserved faithfulness and honesty.

Bree shook her head, dismissing these disturbing thoughts, stopped rocking, and tried to clear her mind of the raging jealousy. She leaned forward and tucked her fingers under her chin, praying that she could find a way to concentrate on her client's needs.

"Is twenty-something the magic number?"

Addy shrugged, her shoulder-length hair brushing against her black T-shirt. She studied Bree with chocolate eyes before she smiled. "All the hotties are still in their twenties."

Bree tsked and grabbed hold of her anger. For a split second she considered telling the woman she couldn't help her, but, God as her witness, it was in her blood to meet the challenge, no matter how hard the task, or how stubborn the client. "Well, first of all, that's completely not true. Most twenty year olds are still looking for mama's tit and a good kick in the rear from daddy. If you're looking for someone to coddle, then that's your magic number. But if you're looking for sophisticated, without the price tag, then I suggest we look for an older woman, maybe one in her early to middle thirties."

Addy shook her head against the suggestion. "I'm pretty firm on that age."

Bree ground her teeth, resisting the urge to roll her eyes like a teenager. The woman sitting across from her wouldn't find her soul mate wading through the "I don't know who I am yet, but you can buy me diamonds and furs in the meantime" women. This possible new client was smart, a self-made millionaire, in her early forties, and she needed, deserved, to meet her intellectual equal, not someone to pet and smother in lavish gifts. Bree could spot those a mile away.

Just like I spotted Logan across a crowded room. Jesus, she'd been so edible, so fuckable, standing out like a country hick in the middle of Bel Air. What was she doing now? Finishing what Bree had interrupted?

The thought sent another pang of jealousy churning through her gut, making her hate herself even more. She didn't do jealousy. It wasn't becoming of a smart businesswoman to act with such stupidity, or such immaturity.

When Addy cleared her throat, Bree blinked and quickly switched back to her business persona. She rechecked her notes, plastered a smile on her face, and looked up to meet Addy's puzzled frown. "I'm sorry, you were saying?"

"I asked why you thought a woman in her thirties would be better suited for me." Addy sat back in her chair, a clear indication she was irritated by Bree's lack of attention.

Bree straightened and met her gaze with one of certainty. "Because it's a number to you. You didn't mention that you're more attracted to twenty-something, or that you could carry on a more intelligent conversation. You didn't mention that you seem to be drawn to the younger women, you merely stated it as a number. And numbers, my friend, are just that. Numbers. I well imagine you've worked long and hard to attain your success. Why waste all you've earned on someone who couldn't care less about your sweat, blood, and tears?"

Addy's brow cocked and Bree knew she'd struck the nail home.

When the phone buzzed, Bree pounced on it, thankful for the distraction. "Love Match, how can I help you?" Bree gave Addy an "I have to take this" shrug.

"May I speak with Bree?"

Bree swallowed hard. She'd recognize that voice anywhere…the same raspy breathing as in that coat closet. And it sent delicious sensations rippling through her body.

She squeezed her legs together and swiveled away from Addy, not wanting anyone to see the heat crawling across her cheeks. "This is Bree."

"Hi, um, this is Logan. I was wondering if we could talk."

The sound of her voice was erotic, so in control, yet so fucking detached from that control. Bree wanted to reach down the telephone line and caress those lips, the very ones she remembered all too well pressed against her own.

She knew she ought to hang up, knew she should make her excuses and be done with the whole mess. For crying out loud, she had a client, a wealthy client, sitting across from her, waiting impatiently for Bree to finish her call. A client who was moments away from barging out of her office if Bree didn't bring their meeting to a satisfactory conclusion so she could sign on the dotted line.

Yet, she couldn't turn back. She cradled the phone deeper into the crook of her neck and swiveled the chair completely around to face the window. This wasn't proper behavior for the businesswoman she'd made of herself. She knew as much, though her body wasn't listening to her mind. Her body was rebelling, slicking juices between her thighs in remembrance of all the things she wanted Logan to do to her.

"Well, I have a client right now." Bree wanted to clamp her mouth shut. Those words implied that if she didn't have a client, she'd have a conversation with Logan.

Fact was, they didn't have anything to talk about. Nothing at all. She'd interrupted a very heated situation in Logan's studio, a situation she should have never been near to begin with.

What in the hell had led her there anyway? Curiosity? Lust? A need to fuck, to be fucked? Either way, she should hang up the phone.

"Have dinner with me."

Bree smiled, despite herself. A giddiness, along with

waves of anxious anticipation, washed over her. She knew she was hanging on Logan's every word, desperate for the sound of her voice.

Jesus, since when did she act so desperate? Never, that's when. "I don't think so."

"Why? Are you afraid you'll lose control and kiss me again?" The humor in Logan's voice thickened and she chuckled.

"Excuse me? I most certainly did not kiss—" Suddenly remembering she wasn't alone in the room, Bree whirled around to face Addy, who smiled like the cat that'd swallowed the canary.

Addy rose from her chair and tapped her watch while Bree covered the mouthpiece. "I'm intrigued by your answer. I have a meeting but will call you later."

Bree nodded her thanks and gave her an apologetic smile, then mouthed, "Thank you."

The door closed behind Addy and Bree's mind reeled with the spiteful things she wanted to scream at Logan before she severed the conversation. She couldn't. Truth was, she wanted to continue talking, to let Logan's voice seduce her, even if it dragged her deeper into purgatory and cost her a valuable client—the very one who'd politely excused herself.

"But you wanted to." Logan interrupted her concentration on the now closing door.

Bree couldn't argue. It was the truth. She'd wanted to so bad—had wanted so much more, though not near as much as she wanted right this very second.

Confused by the knot tying her gut into painful cramps, Bree relaxed into the chair. "What could we possibly have to talk about?"

"Nothing, a lot—that kiss…the way you shot out of

my apartment today." Logan sighed. "Have dinner with me, Bree. I want to smell you again."

With her judgment flying through the window, Bree smiled, every inch of her body heating with Logan's words. Jesus Christ, she was going to have dinner with a woman she should stay far, far away from, and she knew it…and knew it was stupid. Where in God's name was her control? Vanished into thin air at the first sound of Logan's voice. "There's nothing we could discuss over dinner that we can't discuss right now."

"True, but I can't very well taste you over a phone line, now can I?"

Heat ignited between her thighs and Bree had to squirm to ease the pain. "There won't be any smelling, or tasting, or anything of the sort, Ms. Logan Delaney."

"You're going to deprive me of finishing our kiss after we were so rudely interrupted? Don't you think you owe me?"

"Owe you? How could I possibly owe you?"

Logan chuckled. "Because it was your assistant who broke our erotic spell. But for her we might have finished what we started then and there. Besides, you want to kiss me again. Admit it."

Bree grinned. "You're wrong, stud. I have no desire to kiss you again."

"Ahh. You've wounded my heart, both with your words and with your lie."

The silence that followed was more nerve-wracking than the sound of her voice. Bree tapped her nails on the desk, wishing she hadn't played hard to get. Truth was, she wanted that dinner, and that damn kiss. She wanted anything Logan had to offer right now, as sick as the fact was.

"Have dinner with me, Bree. It's important to me."

Bree drew in a sound of relief, though it came out like the sounds of exasperation. “Okay, fine, I’ll have dinner with you, but under one condition—we go as friends, and you will keep your hands to yourself. Understood?”

“I understand it, but I’ll make no promises. Besides, you’ll kiss me, and you’ll do it because you’ve thought of nothing else.”

“Friends, Logan, or I don’t go at all.” For crying out loud, she was going to kiss Logan Delaney again…and she fucking knew it.

Logan chuckled. “Aye aye, ma’am. Seven at Limonia?”

“Make it seven thirty. I have a late meeting.”

“Then it’s a date. Oh, and if it’s not too much bother, could you pick me up at my apartment? My best friend’s taking my car for a few hours tonight, but she’s promised to deliver it to the restaurant before dinner’s over.”

Bree smiled. “That old trick of ‘I need a ride home’ won’t get me in your bed, tiger.”

Logan laughed, a sound so stimulating Bree had to close her eyes against the onslaught. “Well, Ms. One Track Mind, who said I wanted to get you in my bed?”

The silence that followed her words was overpowering. Bree opened her eyes and stared at the closed door, knowing full well that’s exactly where she wanted to be…in Logan’s bed. “Okay, it’s a deal.”

“I’ll wait with bated breath for your arrival, and our next kiss.”

The line went dead.

Bree pulled the receiver away from her ear and stared at it. Her spine pricked with goose bumps to know Logan would do that very thing…would be waiting, eyes for only her, and that Bree would flush all over as soon as she laid eyes on Logan once again. Sick with herself for missing Logan already, Bree hung up the phone and reached for her cell. She was a sick person all right.

Now she had to call off her date with Natalie.

❖

Logan propped her elbows on her knees and stared at the phone still held tight in her grasp.

Where in the hell had that invitation come from? Dinner? Since when did she invite women out? Hell, she didn't have to. They flocked to her door, where they came in a flurry of erotic gasps and shrill screams when she wrenched an orgasm from their bodies soon after.

Did she want to expel an explanation for what Bree had witnessed earlier? An explanation she didn't owe anyone, especially to a woman she barely knew. If that wasn't the reason, then why?

She dropped the phone into the cradle, gave a sigh, and avoided Paula's penetrating stare. Her best friend was known for setting Logan straight with her meaningful expressions. She'd raced to Logan's aid an hour ago, even stood with her across the street in the bookstore while waiting for Penny to escort herself from Logan's apartment, even mocked her like only a best friend could for giving up a piece of ass as fine as Penny's.

"We're having dinner…tonight." Logan forked her fingers through her hair and leaned back against the cushions.

"You know, I *am* in the same room with you, and I'm not deaf. Tell me something I don't know, like why you're bothering to dine her before you take her home to fuck her." Paula curled her legs under her to sit Indian style. "Could my best friend have suddenly developed a conscience?"

Logan looked up. "What's that supposed to mean? Of course I have a damn conscience."

Paula cocked her brow. "The time you moved the kitten out of the road doesn't count because you were only doing it to impress the women watching you from the sidewalk, nor does the time you gave all your change to the homeless man."

"The change was weighing my pockets down and the kitten was too damn cute to be road kill." Paula did make a good point; she'd only saved the damn kitten to woo the women, and scored herself a fuck in the process.

However, simply because she didn't go out of her way to smother people in affection didn't make her a monster, or any less a person with a heart. She really cared about the world around her and treated people with as much respect as they gave her.

When Paula angled her head, Logan rolled her eyes. "Fine, I did it to win a fuck. So what? I have needs, too."

"Yeah, okay, whatever you say, but you didn't answer the question."

Logan looked toward the windows dominated by the red brick building across the alley. She didn't have the answers, nor did she have an inkling of why she needed—no, wanted—to take Bree to dinner. To fuck her? Of course. The need to feel Bree quiver beneath her weight was almost painful, but she could do that without the price tag from a fancy restaurant. Something else was nagging at her, something she couldn't ignore.

And sitting here fretting over it wasn't getting her any

closer to the answers, or helping her get ready for a date in less than two hours.

She pushed off the couch and made her way to the shower, praying the hot steam would douse some of the flame created from the memories of the kiss she shared with Bree…or the one she wanted to steal tonight. God, how she wanted this woman. Had there ever been another she wanted with such a vengeance?

If she had to be honest with herself, the answer was no. She couldn't remember a time she'd wanted to be close to someone, to smell them, to gently caress them. Without a doubt, she wanted to tear Bree apart…the way she was falling apart on the inside right now.

While the hot water jetted against her skin, Paula spoke from just inside the door. "So, I'm still taking your car, right?"

"Yes, but it better be in the parking lot when I'm done dining my night's piece of ass."

"What, and give up your excuse for her to take you home? You sound mighty sure of yourself considering she's a lot more savvy than the squealing models you normally bring home."

Logan snickered at her statement, recalling Bree's response. "That won't work on this one."

Paula chuckled. "I think the pleasure planner is going to make you work your ass off to get in her pants."

Logan ducked under the spray to rinse her hair, and mentally agreed.

Bree would definitely make her work for it, but Lord save them both when she finally got the gorgeous vixen in bed. And she would do just that.

Tonight.

CHAPTER SIX

Logan huffed and stripped off yet another pair of slacks, finally settling on the loose-fitting jeans she'd started with. She looked at the clock, her nerves suddenly jumping to see how little time she had left before Bree arrived.

Donning a pair of tan loafers, she took a calming breath and surveyed her reflection in the full-length mirror. "Okay, easy does it." She addressed the image sternly. "There's absolutely no reason to be acting like a total moron. You've been on a date before. You've wined and dined many beautiful women in the past, so stop acting like an inexperienced teenager about to get your first French kiss."

The homily did little to soothe her jagged nerves. Bree was in a different league from any of her previous dates, both in class and temperament. For a start, she'd never craved total submission from any of her other dates like she did from Bree. Even though they'd barely kissed, she knew, without doubt, that sex between them would be mind-blowingly awesome and it couldn't come soon enough for her—like as soon as Bree walked through the door. Logan closed her eyes to trap the vision of Bree's naked body spread-eagled over the couch while she lapped her. A sudden rush of molten heat drew a gasp from her lips along with the involuntary pressure of her hand against her pussy.

When the door buzzed, she practically threw herself against the wall to steady her knees. What the fuck was wrong with her all of a sudden?

She gulped down indecision swirling through her brain and pushed away from the wall to stare at the array of clothing spread across the bed and floor. No. She turned her back on the discarded garments—she didn't have time to change her mind again about tonight's attire.

With as much grace as she could muster, she shucked into an overshirt and made her way to the living room to buzz Bree into the building.

A final sweep of the room proved she'd covered all the incriminating evidence reminding her of her morning with Penny, and cleaned as much as possible, so she tapped down her anxious nerves and opened the door to wait. The staccato tap-tap of heels on wood did little to suppress the fire suddenly flaming out of control between her thighs. Any second, Bree was going to be in view, wearing only God knew what.

Logan held her breath as Bree started up the stairs from the second floor landing, her face tilted toward Logan's door with wide-eyed anxiety.

When she saw Logan, she smiled…and desire flickered across her expression. She made it to the top and Logan finally remembered to breathe.

With a control she never knew she possessed, Logan resisted reaching for her. She wanted nothing more than to fling Bree against the hallway wall and fuck her standing up, then bend her over the couch and start over again.

When Bree licked her lips, Logan flew apart and swallowed hard. Desire flowed through her body, gathering momentum as she stared down Bree's entire body. She looked edible, like a delicious confection of rich dark and white chocolate, in her cream-colored linen slacks and tight brown silk blouse cut to show off her cleavage. Her nipples strained against the fabric of an obviously too thin bra, teasing Logan with their puckered hardness.

Suppressing the desire to drag Bree into the room, because if she touched her, she wouldn't know how to let go, Logan merely gestured for her to enter. "Welcome to Logan's loft." She gave a smile and followed Bree inside, taking in the sway of her ass, knowing from the looks of those tight cheeks, they'd fit perfectly in her hands while she rode Logan's face.

Bree casually looked around the room then rushed to the closest wall dominated by her canvases. Of course, they weren't the body art Logan painted to pay the bills, but rather her own imaginations—artwork that'd probably never see the air outside her apartment again.

"Wow, these are yours?" Bree's eyes sparkled as she stepped closer to a purple and orange abstract and read the signature. "They're absolutely amazing."

Logan smiled, her head starting to swim with the compliment. Something about the words coming from Bree made her believe them as truth. "I call them my doodle arts. That's all they're good for."

Bree whipped around as if slapped. "Are you kidding me? They're incredible! Why don't you participate in art shows, or, with this number, start up an exhibition of your own? These would be grabbed up faster than you could paint them."

Logan shook her head. "I already entered them in a show, once, two years ago. I sold just one painting to someone I knew, who I assumed only bought it because she felt sorry for me. No one else seemed interested in the raw, bright colors. Though people did stop and stare."

Bree turned back. "That's because everyone's afraid of the newbies…the starving artists, so to speak. They're my favorite. Over the years I've collected quite a few stunning pictures from young artists who've now become quite famous." She fingered the edge of the canvas, almost absentmindedly, gliding slowly up and down. Heat swarmed into Logan's pussy as she imagined those fingers teasing an orgasm from her. "It's a rush to see if they'll make it in the cut-throat competition."

Logan was shocked at her words, mainly because they were so true. For most new artists, it was live or die. If not for her inheritance, or the body art for the rich and famous, she'd be numbered among them—groveling for every dime she could get her hands on.

Bree moved farther down the wall, touching some pieces, stopping to linger in front of others with her head cocked to the side, until she made it to the farthest wall where Logan's grandmother's photographs were framed. The outer edges of each one housed her grandfather's articles that went along with each photograph.

When Bree let out a squeal, Logan startled and followed her gaze. "Holy mother of God, Adeline, of Malcolm and Adeline, the dynamic duo." She squeezed closer to the frame as if the mere contact was electrifying. Her eyes glowed with awe. "How in the fuck did you get your hands on these originals? I'd give my left breast for one of these. Hell, who am I kidding, I'd fuck the devil himself."

Logan stared for several seconds, unsure if the lump in her throat had suddenly formed because she missed her grandparents so badly, or the fact that someone actually remembered them.

She glanced back at the photograph. "She's my grandmother."

Bree's mouth sagged open as she whirled around to face Logan. "No way…no fucking way!" She held her hand to her heart. "Are you serious?"

Logan nodded and stepped closer, her body taking control over her screaming mind. When Bree's eyes widened, it only fueled the uncontrollable fire.

Bree took a step back until her spine pressed against the brick wall. Her chest heaved, her lips automatically parting, and every bit of her posture screamed for Logan to kiss her.

"Very serious. I never joke about family." Logan dropped her gaze to Bree's lips, then lower to watch her chest rise and fall. Those gorgeous breasts called her with every heave. Emotions churned her gut like debris in the eye of a tornado. She wanted to lower her lips to Bree's, wanted to tear at her clothes until silky flesh met her fingertips and then ravish her with her lips, fingers, and tongue. She crooked her finger under Bree's chin and tilted her head back. "You smell delicious."

"Logan, I…"

Logan moved closer until her lips were mere centimeters from Bree's. "I want you to kiss me, Bree. And I want you to want to."

Bree swallowed, then whispered, "Stop trying to seduce me."

Logan turned her head back and forth, feathering her lips across Bree's. "Is that what I'm doing?"

"Yes." The word was nothing more than a breathless pant.

"Are you going to kiss me?" Logan pulled back.

Bree struggled for control with a deep breath, then cleared her throat. "No." She squeezed out of Logan's confinement and quickly turned back to the picture. "I... she, I mean, your grandmother, Adeline, and...I mean, your grandparents were awesome."

Logan listened to the stuttered words. She'd shaken this sexy put-together woman, and liked the sounds of her falling apart. She sounded just like Logan felt—like a frenzied disaster.

"I've read every article your grandparents ever published. My favorite is the family vacation they took with Adele Frazer and Grant Tyler. The photographs of their children frolicking in the ocean as if their parents weren't the hottest couple to ever hit the silver screen were absolutely adorable." She looked over her shoulder at Logan. "Your grandparents were amazing and touched people's hearts."

Logan couldn't tear her gaze away from those lips... wanted desperately to touch them. "That they did." She finally succeeded in looking away to stare at the photographs. "This is just the beginning of what I have planned to honor their creations, though I've been told what I have in mind is impossible to accomplish."

"Why's that?" Bree walked further down the wall, angling her head back to look at the photographs higher up on the ten-foot walls.

Logan closed the gap between them but stopped just short of pressing her body against Bree's back. "I want to convert the key dots on the old presses into the form of letters, then combine his articles into her photographs." She took a deliberate breath to inhale Bree's exotic aromas. "You smell fruity, like ripe peaches—you smell like you need sex."

Bree stiffened and slowly turned around, automatically focusing on Logan's lips. "You're doing it again."

"Am I?" Logan whispered, pleading with herself not to pin Bree against the wall. The need was ripping her in two.

Bree backed up then took a step sideways to disconnect the possibility of touching Logan. "The presses are still downstairs? Must be awesome being you. You live in a shrine to two of the most fabulous people I never knew. Must get you lots of fucks, huh?"

Logan laughed, and really wanted to tell her that she never normally confessed who her grandparents were, or that her dream was to honor their magazine, though wanting that dream and attempting to reach it were worlds apart lately. Hell, the only people she'd shared that desire with were her agent and Paula, who both insisted she was wasting her time on such nonsense, which was possibly why she'd all but given up hope.

Why had she felt compelled to share it with Bree?

She knew the answer as soon as Bree turned back around and gently dragged her finger along the edge of another frame, putting space between them. The world had passed by and forgotten all about her grandparents and their legacy.

But Bree hadn't.

CHAPTER SEVEN

With a last lingering look at photographs she'd never get to see again, Bree turned away. "We'd better get moving. It's getting late and we don't want to lose our table."

Unable to stand another second of torment in the private presence of Logan, whose eyes kept burning a hole through her, mind fucking her, she led the way to the door leaving Logan to follow in her wake, though her slow steps only proved she was purposefully stalling.

Halfway down the stairs, Bree wanted to turn around so bad, to let Logan do all the things those eyes promised, but she couldn't. It was wrong, and she knew it. Though why, she didn't truly understand.

She wasn't cheating, well, maybe technically, she was.

Natalie knew as well as she did that their commitment didn't exist beyond the bedroom, so truly, was that considered cheating?

Shaking her head to swipe away the unanswerable questions, Bree led the way to her car parked on the now deserted street. Trouble was, the small confinement of her vehicle only proved more devastating than the large open living room. Logan was too close, and she smelled so fucking good, like musk, and acrylic…and sex.

Gripping the steering wheel tighter, Bree concentrated on the route to the restaurant, daring tiny glances at Logan along the way. Her hair looked like her stint with the hair dryer was done without means of a brush, and her clothes resembled those she'd been wearing at the auction.

How was it possible that a woman could look so damn sexy with her hair all amok and wearing nothing more than a wifebeater with an unbuttoned overshirt? It should be a sin, yet Bree wanted nothing more than to crawl inside that shirt then rip it from her body.

The image made her cringe. Since when did women like Logan attract her? She always went for the smooth sophisticated type like Natalie. Women like her were the ones who turned her head and made her weak with need. Weren't they? The wetness against her thong proved this theory was no longer true. The slickness between her legs needed satisfaction—and she wanted that relief from Logan, right now.

After what felt like hours, she finally pulled against the curb of a well-known Italian restaurant. Without waiting for Logan, she exited the car and practically threw the keys to the valet before darting inside the thankfully crowded lobby.

She inhaled a sigh of relief until Logan moved close behind her and whispered, "I requested the darkest corner."

Their bodies touched. Bree stiffened as desire rippled down her spine. An uncontrollable need took over. She wanted nothing more than to turn and fall into Logan's tight arms, to tame her like a wild mustang, tearing at her until they both whimpered with relief. Instead, she stepped out of the closeness to steady her ragged breaths. This night was already proving to be a huge mistake.

The host led them to a table tucked against the, God forbid, darkest wall.

When Bree ducked into the booth, Logan squeezed in right beside her. “Don’t want you lonely in this big ol’ booth all by your lonesome.” That damn cute dimple formed in the corner of one cheek when she smiled.

Bree swallowed and took a sip of water to cool her throat. Logan was too close, way too fucking close. She scooted across the seat, but Logan followed until there was nowhere left to go and she was trapped tight against the corner wall. Bree inhaled deeply, savoring Logan’s unique musky scent, and fought the overwhelming urge to give in to the insidious voices playing tug-of-war with her emotions. She picked at the white linen napkin with nervous fingers until she’d scrunched it into a tight ball.

“So, tell me about this dating service of yours.” Logan turned slightly and focused all her attention on Bree.

Bree wanted to tell her to stop looking at her, to stop seducing her—wanted to scream for her to fuck her right here on the table. Instead, she sighed and dug her fingers deeper into the napkin in an attempt to sooth her frazzled nerves. “I like to think of myself as a matchmaker.” Bree smiled, feeling more comfortable talking about her work. “I offer a very personal service, something different from the norm, tailored exactly to my client’s requirements. Consider it a dating service with a kick.”

“*Strike a flame that burns forever*. I like that slogan. Is that what you do for your clients, find their true love?”

Logan’s lips beckoned Bree, moving so damn seductively.

That smile formed on her lips again and Bree fell into a hypnotic trance. She struggled to remember what the question was.

"Um, yes, that's exactly what I do."

Logan rubbed her thigh with a single fingertip. "How can you possibly know two people are a perfect match?"

Bree closed her eyes, the feather-light touch of that finger moving higher and higher, circling and teasing. She opened her eyes. "Instinct, I suppose…I just know."

"Are you psychic?"

Bree licked her suddenly parched lips as Logan's hand reached the top of her leg, her fingers dipping into the vee of her thighs. "My mom says I am. But I'm not." Beyond desperate for relief, she parted her legs, allowing cool air to caress her heat. She wanted to pull Logan's hand against her pussy and delve against it until an orgasm shattered.

"Sure wish you could read minds."

Bree narrowed her eyes, suddenly aware they were in public, no matter how dim the lighting at their table was. "Why do you say that?"

Logan leaned over and pressed her lips against Bree's ear. Her fingers dipped with the movement, pressing firmly against Bree's pussy, before she whispered, "If you could read my mind right now, you'd see me throwing you on this table and opening your legs like an erotic novel so I could taste you, and make you bellow out my name as you come all over my mouth."

Bree sucked in a breath and shoved Logan's hand away. She straightened against the booth and smoothed her hair down, completely shocked at her lack of self-control. What the fuck was she doing allowing Logan to seduce her so easily, and where the hell was she getting the power to do so? Where was her fucking self-control? She was always in control, always.

She cleared her throat and took another sip of water. "Okay, enough playing. I only came here because…" When

Logan gave her a skeptical grin, Bree knew she didn't have the answer.

For the first time in her life, she didn't have an answer to a simple question. Why was she here? There was no logical explanation, and the wider Logan's smile became, the more confused Bree became, and the more the question nipped at her mind.

"Because you wanted to kiss me again?"

Everything crashed through her mind at once, her needs, her wants, tying her in knots with indecision, and bittersweet regret. Logan was an artist who whored herself out for fame and fortune and Bree was a genuine matchmaker who devoted every waking minute to making others happy.

They were like oil and water. So what the hell was she doing sitting in a booth next to this intoxicating wench when she could be on her back screaming Natalie's name right now?

When the waitress appeared, Bree rattled off her order and sat back to let her thoughts unravel. She was in a dead-end relationship with a woman who probably hadn't wondered why she'd called off their dinner date, who was probably, at this very second, curled up with her client files…not sparing Bree a single thought, completely unconcerned about what she was doing tonight, or even who she was with.

They didn't have a relationship. They never had.

How had she gotten herself into such a mess? Worse, why was she letting it dominate her life?

Bree forced herself to eat the prime rib, though she pushed the vegetables around on her plate, her appetite draining as her mind reeled with questions, with images of all the things she wanted to do to Logan.

Finally, they both pushed away their half-eaten plates, declined the dessert menu, and settled for coffee, waiting in complete silence until the steaming mugs arrived. Bree sipped the strong fragrant Costa Rican, conscious that she still hadn't achieved what she came here to do. The whole purpose of this evening was to finish this, to get Logan off her back and out of her system once and for all.

Despite her good intentions, she'd only succeeded in digging herself deeper into the quagmire of sexual turmoil.

After some minor chitchat to keep from saying nothing at all, Bree finally followed Logan from the restaurant praying all the way to the parking lot that her car would be delivered as promised. She bit back a grateful sigh when Logan pointed out a silver Beemer parked a few bays away from her Lotus.

Needing to get away, to think, to fall apart, Bree darted to her own car with Logan close behind.

"Thanks for dinner." Bree beeped the car unlocked then reached for the handle.

Logan stepped in behind her, blocking her from opening the door. "It was my pleasure."

Bree's insides heated with the whisper of the fire against her back from Logan's body weight. Her knees almost buckled with raging emotions and she leaned against the car for support.

When Logan gently tugged her arm, Bree came undone. Terrified to turn around, to be hypnotized by those eyes once again, yet yearning with all of her being for a few precious moments in those arms.

Bree slowly turned in Logan's grasp and stared into dark eyes smoldering with need. Logan leaned down, hesitant, as if expecting Bree to resist. If she could hear the hammering of her heart, Logan would have known she was without power to resist those lips.

She closed her eyes and waited. Logan sucked on her

lower lip before sliding her tongue against Bree's in a slow, gentle thrust. Reckless need curled tight and hot in her belly. She flung her arms around Logan's neck and wove her fingers into thick hair. Their mouths locked, tongues struggling for territory inside each other's mouths.

Wild, breathless, and out of control, Bree clung to Logan like her very life depended on their proximity. Logan cupped her ass, squeezing and molding the cheeks to fit the palm of her hand before she crooked Bree's legs over her hips and ground against her in hard thrusts.

Bree moaned into Logan's mouth, fisting handfuls of her hair, pumping against her in desperate thrashes.

Her mind was a void, and her body was so hot it was painful. She'd never felt anything like it. God, she wanted Logan, needed her so badly it bit her to the bone.

Logan wove her hands up her back, hooked her hands over Bree's shoulder, then used the leverage to slam into Bree's pussy.

Bree slung her head back, her arms wrapped tightly around Logan's shoulder, her nails clawing through her shirt.

Logan hooked her mouth around the flesh of Bree's throat, then eased her from the door to the hood of the car. Pushing her roughly back, she fell on top of Bree, kneeing her legs apart, moaning out her name, driving Bree into chaotic need.

Bree felt vulnerable beneath her weight, naked and exposed to the world. Jesus, she was practically fucking this woman in public, and somehow she didn't care. It felt natural, like a wild side of her had been unleashed.

She locked her ankles behind Logan's back and met her hurried thrusts.

"I'm so fucking out of control when I'm near you."

Logan slammed her hips against Bree then grabbed her arms and forced them down to the hood. She circled her hips against Bree's weeping crotch. "I want to be inside you, Bree. Please."

Bree wanted that so bad it made her bite back a sob. But she couldn't. Heaven help her, she couldn't. She jerked forward until Logan slid off her body, staring at her with an expression of heated turmoil, eyes full of want and confusion. Bree was positive that same expression rested on her own face. She'd never needed anyone so much in her life. Fuck, what the hell was happening to her?

In truth, she was unraveling by the second, losing every vestige of the control she'd perfected throughout her life. She'd never allowed anybody this close before, yet with a single kiss, Logan had snatched it all away.

Bree swiped the back of her hand across her mouth and pushed Logan aside. She scrambled weakly down the side of her car then wrenched open the door. With barely a pause, she dropped into the driver's seat, feeling too hot, too wild. She couldn't stand to drive away while Logan stood by the car, her lips glimmering from their kiss, her eyes making promises Bree desperately wanted her to keep.

Bree jerked her gaze away, knowing another second would have her out of the car and spread-eagle across the hood once again, begging Logan to make her come, to scream her name.

With a sob trapped in her throat, she revved the engine and peeled away from Logan.

Chapter Eight

Bree headed for the sanctuary of Natalie's condo as if the hounds of hell were after her. She weaved precariously through the late evening traffic barely registering if the lights were red, yellow, or green, her mind overflowing with incredibly hot, horny images of Logan and all the things she wanted to do to her—all the things she could have done to her.

This evening had proved a complete failure. Bree forced herself not to think about the consequences of her actions. She wanted answers, wanted a solution or antidote to the feelings her brief encounter with Logan had stirred up, but the longer she spent with Logan the more convinced she became there weren't any answers, and right now she didn't give a shit. She only wanted satisfaction.

When her cell phone chirped, she delved in her purse for the Bluetooth, then pushed it onto her ear. "Hello?"

"I can still smell you," Logan whispered, her raspy words soaking Bree instantly.

Her gut churned and she gripped the steering wheel against the onslaught of sweet pain. Jesus, she wanted to turn the car around and finish what they'd started. She needed Logan, though she knew she shouldn't. She needed her to put out this raging fire, the one that should have never been started to begin with.

Yet she knew it was wrong to want this way, to need this bad, to yearn with every ounce of her body. Godammit, it was so fucking wrong.

"Logan, I can't..."

"I can still feel you. You wanted me." Logan's whispered words sounded urgent, and then she panted and Bree could feel her nerves unraveling.

"You have to stop, Logan!"

A soft moan met Bree's ears and she leaned toward the steering wheel and squeezed her legs together to quell the unbearable inferno tearing at her crotch like invisible steel-hot fingers.

"I need you, Bree. Oh God, you have no idea all the things I want to do to you." Logan's heavy breathing assaulted her mind and Bree squeezed her legs tighter, knowing all she had to do was hang up the phone to sever the sound of Logan's self-satisfaction.

She didn't even have the power to do that. Logan had made her weak, was making her weaker by the second. Instead of shutting out the sounds like she knew she should, Bree listened to the exotic moans, to the sounds of Logan's haggard breathing...while she unraveled on the inside.

She could barely drive, consumed by the sounds—all the sounds she wanted to pull from Logan with her tongue and fingers. She could still feel Logan's hard frame pressing against her chest, pinning her against the metal, grinding and pumping against her.

When a car hooted and zoomed around her in the slow lane, Bree came to her senses, weaved in behind it, and cut her speed. Probably in the nick of time since she was in serious danger of wrecking the car if she didn't stop thinking, wanting, needing…or listening to Logan.

She pulled into the first vacant parking lot and shoved the shifter into neutral. With the parking brake on and the motor idling, she swallowed hard. This was absolutely ridiculous, this feeling, these emotions. Had she ever felt them before?

With a sigh, she knew she hadn't. It was lust, and it was causing her to react irrationally, and even the knowledge didn't stop her from wanting Logan, yearning for the nutrition her body craved, that only Logan could feed her right now.

"I want to taste you…and drive my fingers inside you. I want to hear you come, Bree."

Bree opened her mouth to tell her she wanted the same things, only that they could never have those things because she was taken by another, but Logan's demanding moan stopped her.

"Logan, please…I can't…"

"Come back, Bree. I need you pumping beneath me."

Bree screwed her eyes shut and Logan's virtual image was right there, shoving her against the car, her body levering Bree off her feet with hard, demanding grinds. She let go of her death grip on the steering wheel and pushed her hand between her legs.

"Bree…I want to fuck you so hard. Turn around, I beg you."

Bree opened her eyes and looked around. Cars passed her by, their lights illuminating the dark pavement, oblivious to the car idling in the dark parking lot. She unsnapped her slacks and slid her hand inside. She was so wet. Logan was drenching her with just her voice, with those enticing, seducing moans.

"Keep talking…keep moaning. Make me come, Logan."

Bree felt a pang of guilt right before she slid two fingers inside herself, then she moaned and the guilt was shoved to the darkest recess of her mind.

"I sure hope you're pulled over somewhere."

"Seduce me, dammit." Bree flicked her wet finger against her clit and shoved her body against the seat.

"Tell me what you're doing to yourself."

"I'm so wet, Logan."

"Fuck…me too. Please meet me at my apartment. I need to feel you."

Bree shoved her fingers inside herself, too far gone to stop now. "I can't…I just can't." She wanted to scream that she had a girlfriend, that she was waiting for Bree right now, that she wanted so bad to do just that…to go to Logan and fuck her.

"Yes, you can, baby."

Bree shoved her fingers deeper, pushing against the floorboard with every thrust. "Please, Logan."

Logan gave a resigned sigh. "You're wet, Bree, for me. Fuck yourself over those fingers."

Bree did, drilling her fingers deep inside herself.

"Close your eyes, Bree."

Bree did as she was told, shutting out the darkness of the reality around her.

"You can feel me, pressing that tight body against your car, grinding against you, wanting you. I'm working my hand inside your pants, further, moving against your wet pussy."

Bree worked herself over her probing fingers, the ball of her palm working against her clit, seeing everything Logan was describing for her. She wanted to be in Logan's arms, coming by her hands, screaming out her name. It was so wrong, and so right.

"My fingers slide inside you, deep, fucking you, lifting you off your feet with every hard thrust…positioning you over my hips, deeper still, and you want me so bad it hurts, and you need to come, and cry, and scream…" Logan panted, her voice a raspy whisper.

"Oh…I need you inside me, Logan." Bree thrashed over her fingers, eyes sealed shut, body tight with the oncoming orgasm.

"I am inside you, and you're soaked, clinging to me, and fucking yourself…up and down, you pummel yourself over my fingers."

"I'm gonna…" Bree felt the hot sting of her insides, clenching, unclenching, tightening around her fingers in hard pulses.

"Come with me, Bree," Logan whispered.

The plea tore Bree over the edge. "I'm coming, Logan. Oh, fuck, I'm coming!"

And then Logan was gasping for breath, and the sounds of her breathless groans filled the airways…and Bree was falling apart right beside her.

By the time Bree made it to Natalie's apartment, she was beside herself with need, and guilt, and still unsatisfied. She was so horny from replaying her orgasm in her car, with Logan coming with her. Jesus, she was in pain. Her body still ached, and her mind was filled to the brink with Logan. And with every step toward Nat's door, she knew she was in the wrong place, that it was unthinkable to allow Natalie to put out Logan's fire. There was only one woman who should put out this inferno. However, she'd come here to seek solace in

Nat's arms, and that, she intended to do. Maybe Nat's arms would get her thoughts back together, would make her feel something she might miss if not in them.

She took a deep breath, switched off the phone, and swept the lingering sounds of Logan coming from her mind before she entered the apartment.

Natalie glanced up from her curled position on the couch and nodded in greeting. "Hi there, gorgeous. Did you have a nice night?"

Bree wanted to pounce on her, tear at her, and then grind against her until she was sated. Yet something stilled her from doing just that. Nat wasn't Logan, and it wasn't fair to let her extinguish someone else's fire.

Besides which, after that cursory greeting Natalie immediately reverted to her normal, aloof, "don't disturb me, I'm buried in work" zone.

Bree sighed and wandered through to the kitchen where she helped herself to a glass of chilled chardonnay from the fridge and downed it without appreciating the subtle vanilla scent or its creamy, peachy, lemony aftertaste. She refilled her glass, poured one for Natalie, and then returned to the living room.

Natalie was so engrossed in her work she didn't even glance up until Bree had crossed the room, pulled the files from her lap, and tossed them onto the floor. Nat's quizzical stare finally focused upon Bree as she straddled her lap.

She wrapped her arms around Nat's neck, desperate for some sign of want, and pulled her closer for a heated kiss, though the kiss did little to compare to the soaked mess caused by Logan's erotic moans.

She should take a shower, should swipe away all evidence that another woman had made her come, even over a phone line.

"Ah, you're in another weird mood." Nat held Bree at arm's length and grinned, but her expression proved she wasn't any more comfortable with this change of routine tonight than she had been last evening.

Guilt plagued Bree. Touching Natalie was wrong. The wrongness swarmed over her, choked her. But the need for relief was more unbearable. She pumped her hips against Nat, wanting more, wanting Logan, knowing it was so fucking wrong.

"I thought you might like a change—something naughty and different." Bree leaned down to capture those luscious cherry lips, but Natalie stopped her with a palm to her chest. "Come take a shower with me."

With Nat's hard stare, Bree knew their relationship was over. Worse, she didn't know how she felt about it. Part of her wanted to jump for joy then race back to Logan. The other was already missing the day-to-day routine, the convenience of having a sexual partner at her disposal.

And then there was the third voice, the one that never steered her wrong, tapping her common sense to tell her this had been over long before tonight. Nat was a great woman, and made an incredible partner, but not for Bree. They were wrong together.

"I think we need to talk." Nat pushed Bree until she rose out of her lap.

Bree knew there wasn't anything left to talk about. It was over, if it'd ever really begun.

How did you compare a fuck partner to a relationship?

You couldn't, and this wasn't a relationship. This was a convenience for each of them.

Bree tingled with anticipation, anxious to get the ending over with, without any bloodshed or recriminations. Then she could do what she really wanted with a clear conscience.

She could crawl into Logan's arms and finish what they'd started, twice.

Nat took several paces, head down, forking her fingers through her hair, before she turned back to Bree with a wooden stare. "Do you love me?"

Bree blinked hard; she hadn't expected such a direct question. And the answer wasn't so straightforward. "Yes—and no."

Nat smiled and nodded. "I feel the same way. I adore your company, in and out of our beds, but love…" She angled her head. "That real, can't live without you for a second love just isn't there between us."

Bree smiled, feeling an enormous weight lifted from her chest. She flipped into friend mode immediately. "I know, and I agree."

Nat crossed back to Bree and took her hands. "Don't get me wrong, I totally loved the sex…so hot, and awesome, but now I need something more. Suddenly, I miss the love, though I don't think I've ever really had it." She leaned forward and dropped a kiss on Bree's cheek. "You're an amazing woman, beautiful, smart, and sexy, and for a long time, I thought you were the one…convinced it would be you."

Bree shook her head and pulled one hand free to caress Nat's cheek. "It's not me, Nat. I'm not the one. I never was, if truth be told, neither one of us could see it. Which doesn't say much for my skill as a matchmaker."

Nat leaned down and placed her forehead against Bree's. "The world wouldn't be right without your intervention. Love stands no chance with you out there searching for it."

Bree hugged her. "I'm only a phone call away if you ever need me."

"And I won't hesitate to dial it." Nat pulled back. "Friends?"

"You bet!" Bree smiled, happy tears threatening.

It was all over, no recriminations or bloodshed. Relieved, Bree hugged Nat again, and when she hugged her back, they were nothing more than friends.

"I'm actually jealous of your matchmaking skills, though I promise not to hire you." Nat winked, and they both laughed.

After a final good-bye, Bree raced to her car, desperate for Logan's touch, desperate to come screaming by her hands.

CHAPTER NINE

Logan lay on her back and wriggled her body beneath the half-ton printing press. She angled the light closer to the screws securing the line of keys and attempted once again to break the tenacious hold that resulted from years of dirt and neglect. Just when she rejoiced with a faint movement, the screwdriver blade slipped out of the slot and her knuckle crashed into metal. The echoes of her bellowed pain rang around the cavernous workshop long after she stuffed her hand in her mouth and slid out from beneath the metal monster.

"Fuck!" She sat up, threw the screwdriver away in frustration, and then examined the gash across the back of her hand that was already oozing blood. "This is useless!"

And it was. She'd been tinkering with these presses for well over a year and still, she'd barely made any progress. It was no wonder she'd almost stopped coming down here. The presses mocked her every time she managed to exchange a single dot or number and, no matter how hard she tried or what little task she accomplished, her ultimate goal seemed to recede further into the distance. Or maybe the ghosts of her grandparents were trying to tell her she was a moron for thinking she could attempt the unthinkable, that she could do what no one believed she could do.

She pressed her back against the wall and glanced at the discarded phone lying close by on the floor. It was late and Bree hadn't called her back, as she'd half expected, hoped, she might. What was she doing right now? Was she lying in the arms of another, sated from multiple orgasms or peacefully asleep, alone, in her own bed, her luscious body wrapped in a sheer nightgown? Ah, Logan sighed, the thought was too arousing to consider.

She couldn't believe she'd masturbated, or that Bree had joined her. Damn if the sounds would forever jolt her to the core with need. It'd been painful, hearing her, unable to hold her when she was coming, unable to make her come. And Bree had heard her desperate cries as well. What the hell had gotten into her? And why was Bree resisting her?

She couldn't swipe the taste and feel of Bree from her mind, and God, how she'd wanted, needed, satisfaction. Even the strong pulses of her orgasm hadn't diminished the yearning still raking hot nails along her pussy.

She wanted Bree so bad it made her ache in places never awakened before. She wanted Bree in her bed, wrapped beneath her, pumping against her, whispering in her ear while she came. Dammit, she wanted Bree in every aspect, in ways she'd never wanted another.

Desperate to get those luscious curves out of her mind, Logan banged the back of her head against the wall then stood, giving the press a silent prayer before she ducked beneath its body once again.

❖

Bree eased the car against the curb, her confusion strong, but her needs even stronger. She slid from the seat and stepped onto the sidewalk, battling the emotional war going on in her mind whether to take the next step or not. Hell! Talk about on the rebound. This must be some sort of record. She'd only split with Natalie half an hour ago and here she was at Logan's door burning up with need, consumed by lust. Could she really trust herself to think straight and make the right decisions?

Once she walked through those doors, there was no turning back, and the game was over. If she went back to the car, she could go home, alone, albeit wet and unsatisfied, but still be the same Bree come morning light.

Who was she kidding? She shook her head and almost snickered at her stupidity. The old Bree was long gone, probably for good. She'd disappeared back at the auction, the second she caught sight of a gorgeous woman across the room who looked like she didn't belong. Her whole life had changed in a matter of minutes, and here, now, the new Bree stood, begging the voice of sanity to tell her what to do.

Hell, she didn't need any fucking voice giving her advice because she knew where her destiny lay. She was going to walk through those doors, and she was going fuck a player who fucked many women for the simple task of hearing them come. Controlling them. Tomorrow, yes, tomorrow, she would deal with the consequences of tonight's actions.

Fluid seeped against her pussy. With a resigned sigh, she stepped to the door and knocked once, then again. The faint sound of jazz was audible behind the door, though it didn't seem to be coming from higher up in Logan's apartment.

Bree tried the knob and it turned, just as she thought it might. She shook her head. Logan seriously needed to remember to lock her doors. There was way too much precious cargo on the first floor to leave it readily available for every burglar in San Francisco.

She stepped into the lobby and closed the door, making sure to lock it behind her then turned toward the music, which came from the partially open door on the first floor.

Her heart slammed against her chest as she poked her head around the door and found herself looking at an antique print workshop almost untouched by time. Framed photographs lined every available wall, stretching high, dipping low, dominating almost every square inch.

She stared in awed amazement as she approached the nearest wall and fingered the edges of the frames, staring, practically drooling, and still wet with need.

When something moved behind her, she whirled around to find Logan rising from behind one of the presses. She was wearing a pair of overalls over nothing more than a white wifebeater. Godammit, it should be a sin for a woman to look that fucking good resembling someone who should be tossing hay with a pitchfork.

And those eyes, staring at her. Logan was going to fuck her like she'd never been fucked before.

For several agonizing seconds, the music stopped, and nothing moved or broke the silence but her ragged breathing. Her feet were rooted to the spot and all her attention focused on Logan, whose sensual expression told her everything she wanted to know.

A new song blared from the speakers of the boom box. The sound galvanized Bree into action. Barely conscious of what drove her, she moved like an athlete out of the starting blocks just as Logan charged toward her.

They crashed into each other, tangled arms and roaming hands, moaning, crying out their need.

Everything felt so right, like this was the way it should be—destined to be.

Logan's tongue forced inside her mouth, stabbing,

exploring, and tasting her. It was the most perfect kiss she'd ever had…the kiss was perfection.

Bree pulled back, her hands searching buttons, rivets, whatever the hell was holding this contraption together. In frustration, she yanked at the denim material while Logan captured her mouth again. Was she just as hungry for their connection? God, she was. Bree could feel it with every swipe of her tongue.

She gave up hope of the overalls, so she grabbed Logan's ass and tugged her closer, circling her hips, and moaning. Heavens above, she wanted Logan inside her, pumping deep, and making her fucking scream louder than she'd ever screamed.

When Logan pulled back, Bree felt lost by her solid form. Then Logan reached forward and her fingers fumbled the tiny pearl buttons on Bree's top, softly, then rough, right before she growled and tore the buttoned seam apart in one yank. Logan's lips parted in a brief smile as Bree's chest heaved, and then her hands closed over Bree's breasts, molding them, thumbing across her nipples through her lace bra until Bree let loose a ragged breath.

"Logan, please!" Bree raked her fingers through her hair, down the nape of her neck.

Logan stood back, her eyes glowing with desire. Bree knew that soon, very soon, their unfinished business would finally be finished. That time couldn't come soon enough. She wanted it so fucking bad she seared with pain, all over her body, inside her body, taking over her mind. Jesus, if she didn't come soon she was going to combust into a wall of fire.

She wrapped her arms around Logan's neck and hooked her other leg around her hip. Logan palmed her ass, holding her weight easily in her arms. She pumped against Bree, driving her out of her mind with a suffering privation. She clung wildly to the woman she wanted to fuck.

"Please fuck me, Logan. I need you inside me." Bree nipped her earlobe, then dipped to her neck, using mouth, tongue, and teeth as her guide, needing the total experience of flesh against flesh.

Logan walked until she slammed Bree against the wall. She drove her hips against Bree in wild jolts, pounding Bree against the hard wall.

She dove back in for another kiss, rubbing Bree's pussy from behind, between her legs. Bree arched backward, desperate for the pressure of those fingers, wild with a need to come.

When Logan lifted her once again, Bree expelled a groan, but didn't break that delicious kiss. She was roughly placed on the edge of one of the machines and she locked Logan between her thighs, her pussy soaked, her body trembling.

Logan shoved her down until her back was pressed against cold metal, then climbed on top of her. "I'm going to fuck you so hard, Bree." She pinned Bree's hands above her head and ducked for her throat, trailing wet kisses along her path, her hot breath feathering against Bree's skin.

Bree released the desperate moan trapped in her throat and wiggled against Logan. "I'm on fire, Logan. Please, I can't take much more."

Logan jerked back as if bitten, staring at Bree with an aroused, yet confused expression on her face. "What the fuck?"

CHAPTER TEN

Logan took several steps back, her lips curled in distaste—the scent of another woman on Bree's skin provoked a raging torrent of anger and jealousy.

She had no right at all to feel anything, let alone jealousy. Yet, she couldn't fight off the biting sting of the green-eyed monster. Bree was hers, or rather, tonight, she wanted her to be…wanted her to be hers, and hers alone. She suddenly felt like a kid with a new toy, and wanted to covet her prized possession, but that sexy package reeked of someone else's scent.

"What's wrong?" Bree sat up and reached for her, her expression begging Logan to come back to finish what they both craved.

"You smell like you've just fucked someone else." Logan felt the sting of her own words, the snarl behind each syllable, and she didn't care. She resisted the urge to scream at Bree, to shake her, and then fuck her until all thoughts of any other woman faded to mist.

Bree's smile only fueled her rage. Logan sucked back a growl.

"It's a long, complicated story, and that relationship is now over." Bree pushed off the press and took a step forward, but Logan stepped back, sure if Bree touched her she'd combust with sexual hunger. Or worse, not care that she'd come at the hands of another woman, and fuck her anyway.

Logan shook her head, mainly to knock the uncharacteristic thoughts from her mind. She didn't do jealousy; it wasn't in her nature. But dammit if she wasn't ready to sling Bree over her knee for a spanking to make her forget the hands that'd just roamed her curves.

Logan clenched her fists. "You just fucked another woman, and now you want me to fuck you as a consolation prize because she dumped you?"

Bree gasped and her eyes widened. "No, that's not…let me explain."

Logan suddenly wanted to retract every word, conscious that she'd just stepped over the imaginary boundary. "I don't want to hear your fucking explanations. Do I look that desperate?"

Bree's glare turned steely and her eyes filled dangerously fast with hatred. "Desperate? You dare to call me desperate? So it wasn't you I interrupted on your knees in front of Penny Carrow?" Bree closed the space between them, her fiery glare pinning Logan in her spot. "I don't recall ever being desperate enough to fuck a client. You're nothing more than an artistic whore."

Logan opened her mouth to defend herself, and then realized she didn't have a defense. It was true. She'd fucked her clients—many of them. Was it to keep them coming back, to keep her pockets filled with the thick tips they seemed eager to stuff in her faded Levi's? She was fooling herself if she tried to believe anything different. Had she done it for the fuck, or for the fame? Hadn't she fucked hundreds of women, clients or not? Would it matter either way to Bree to hear that pathetic excuse? Bree would only believe the picture painted before her, and Logan couldn't blame her. Bree was right. She was desperate, but for what, she didn't know. It sure as hell wasn't the free pussy delivered to her doorstep by the rich and famous, or anyone else for that matter.

"You're a coward and a disgrace to your grandparents. You should be ashamed of yourself." Bree spun on her heels but Logan grabbed her arm. The mere mention of her grandparents had her anger boiling over into rage.

She whirled Bree around to face her. "Don't turn this around on me, dammit. You're the one who just left one woman's bed and came looking for another. In my book, that makes you a bed-hopping slut!"

Bree's hand was in motion before Logan ever saw her flinch. At the last second, she deflected the slap, grabbed Bree's wrists and pinned it by her side. "Whoa! Calm down, tiger."

Bree bared her teeth. "You bitch!" And then she leaned forward, closing the gap once again, and her mouth claimed Logan's.

Her tongue delved into Logan's mouth, her hot breath a moaned gush of air as she sealed their mouths together. Logan reacted, everything else suddenly unimportant, her hands groping at Bree, tugging at her clothes in a hasty attempt to feel her flesh. Bree fisted her fingers into Logan's hair, their tongues still exploring and dancing. She tugged Logan's head back and nipped the skin at the hollow of her throat.

Logan let out a pent up cry, unsure what the hell she was doing, being controlled by this little fireball, and loving it.

When Bree shoved away, her eyes glazed with a conflicting mixture of "come fuck me" and "I hate you,"

Logan stumbled on weak knees, adrenaline and pheromones overshadowing any rational thoughts. She made a grab for Bree, but she evaded her.

"Go to hell, Logan Delaney. I'd never be desperate enough to fuck you!" Bree spun around and raced from the workshop before Logan knew she'd moved.

The front door slammed while she stood in shocked silence, staring at the vacant doorframe, her body temperature soaring to unbearable heights.

When she heard Bree's car peel away from the curb, she felt an icy chill as the door of finality slammed in her face. What the hell had she done? She was so close, so damn close, and Bree felt so fucking good. Logan wanted to do things to her body she'd never done before, and she wanted to do them over and over and over, wanted to hear Bree plead and beg for an end to the glorious pleasure.

And that woman was now several blocks away, leaving her a soaked mess and feeling like a complete idiot.

But was she really? Was it wrong to question the stench of another female on a woman she wanted to rip apart with her bare teeth? Hell no!

"Fuck you, too, Bree!" Logan screamed at her empty surroundings, her mind spitting out objections, her body yearning, and her pussy enflamed and throbbing from much needed attention.

Now after feeling the growl of her own words, she felt the bittersweet loneliness. Bree was gone, and Logan knew she'd never return. A woman like her never looked back. Logan knew she'd likely never see her gorgeous face again and she missed her already and wanted her back so bad, so she could do things differently.

She slowly turned around, taking in the scenery of printing presses, her grandmother's photographs with her grandfather's articles circling each. Guilt, slow and steady, reached into her heart and squeezed.

Bree was right. She should be ashamed of herself. Instead of working on the presses, she'd been fucking her clients, and loving it. Instead of finding a way to do what everyone thought was impossible, she'd been whoring herself out, in more ways than one.

Dammit. She'd shoved her dream aside for casual sex and money, and pushed her grandparents to the back of the line behind all the uncaring people. How could she do that?

Because she'd only been thinking of herself, and no one else.

She hung her head in shame. Bree was right. She was a disgrace.

"Stop it, Mom!" Bree swatted at the deck of tarot cards for the twentieth time, shook her head, and gave her mom a "you're not doing a reading on me no matter how many times you try to trick me" glare. "I'm not cutting the cards. Give it up!"

Her mom stepped back, her loose-fitting caftan floating around her body as she moved. "I can't give it up. I'm your mother and you're not talking to me."

Bree stood and walked around to the other side of the card table, eager to finish helping her mother set up for her weekly dinner party so she could get the hell out of here. "I've told you all there is to tell you. We broke up, all very civilized, and by mutual agreement. Nothing more, nothing less—simple and sweet."

Her mother huffed, mock defeat written in the tone. Bree sighed. Just like any mother, hers could spot when she wasn't confiding everything, and sense if something wasn't right in her daughter's perfect little world. Didn't help that her mother always seemed to know when she was lying, or even when she wasn't telling the whole story. Bree shifted uncomfortably under the penetrating scrutiny from those steel gray eyes. That stare would turn her into a blubbering idiot if she didn't get this set-up complete then get out of here and wind her way back to her lonely house. How did her mother always manage to drag the truth out of her, make her confess things with only a stare?

But not tonight. There was no way she'd confess the emotions ripping her apart. Absolutely no way she could explain how she felt about a woman who should have never been able to catch her eye to begin with.

"You'll feel much better if you get it off your chest." Her mother moved to another card table and dropped a deck of tarot cards near the edge.

Bree followed, placing empty glasses beside the plates. A large dish of finger foods already occupied the center of every table—carrots, chips, celery sticks, peanuts, mints, and several bowls of dips. Bree dipped a carrot in the ranch dressing and popped it into her mouth, mainly so she wouldn't have to answer something she'd already answered, even if she hadn't confessed anything about Logan.

Just the mental sound of her name had anger bubbling in Bree. How dare that bitch go off like she had without giving her a chance to explain? Who did she think she was? Her mind tumbled, along with a fresh bout of butterflies in her stomach as she recalled their death grip on one another—how desperate they'd been to fuck each other.

"See, just like that!" Her mother pointed a stiff finger at Bree, dragging her out of her semiconscious world, her pussy heating automatically with the memories. "Your whole aura just changed from dark blue to dark red. You're angry, but aroused." She stepped closer, her straight silver hair kissing the shoulder of her dress. "Someone, or something, has your blood boiling. Someone you want to make love to. Who is it? You sure never wore that pretty color with Natalie."

Bree widened her eyes, hating that her mother could read people so damn easily. Shit! "It's nothing. And it's not arousal! I'm just a little uptight over a new client." She dipped another carrot into the ranch dressing and quickly tossed it into her mouth.

Her mother shifted her weight and propped her fist on her hip. "And now you're lying to the woman who went through thirteen hours of labor pains to push you into this world, who would know her daughter is lying just from the way she shifts her eyes away. The fact that your aura is fluttering like a rainbow helps, too." She grinned, and Bree knew she wouldn't give up without a fight. Her mother was pushy like that and had a way of making Bree crumble under her scrutiny.

When the phone rang, Bree welcomed the intervention, but her mother gave her an "I'm not done with you" stare as she went in search of the receiver.

Bree stared at her retreating back, wondering what color her aura would have been last night while she tugged at Logan, wanting to be inside her, fucking her, listening to her breathless pleas. She knew making love to Logan would have blown her away, would have been unlike any sex she'd ever had, good or bad.

But then what? So what if the sex would be tear-jerking? Did the climax compare to the fact that she'd have been playing the player's game? That once Logan got the goody, she'd vanish? No, it didn't matter. She hadn't cared about the aftermath; she'd only wanted to come screaming by Logan Delaney.

She was a sick person and totally out of her character. This was not who she was or who she wanted to be. She wanted the old Bree back, the one who treasured her morals. Would she ever come back? Would she ever get Logan out of her mind? Would it take fucking her to get that job done?

"Hi, sweetie. Yes, yes, we're all set up and waiting…got a few surprise visitors coming as well." Her mother rattled off in the background. "You won't be disappointed."

Bree smiled as she listened. Her mother was such a natural at matchmaking that whoever her victim was tonight would definitely go home a happy woman, and all out of the kindness of her mother's heart. All she'd accepted were friendly hugs and homemade dishes, and seldom a lunch out.

Her mind shifted to Natalie. Had she done the right thing? Without a doubt, she knew she had. It didn't help she was still horny and in need of satisfaction, something she wouldn't be right now in Nat's familiar arms. But their relationship had run its course and died with nothing to hold it together other than the familiarity of a safe fuck without emotional strings—a place for fantastic sex when time allowed. Wasn't that a good enough reason for her to seek love elsewhere?

She balked at the question, a tiny gasp escaping her lips as answers flooded her mind.

Love? Hadn't she wanted that once before? Where had her quest for love vanished to?

Buried under years of hard work building up her business and, if she were honest, her fear of commitment, of letting down her defenses and placing her emotional well-being in the hands of another person.

"Oh, dear, he's a hunk, and such a gentleman. He can't wait to meet you." Her mother continued.

With her mother's happy smile, light bulbs flashed in Bree's mind.

How could she possibly earn a living finding everyone else's soul mate while hers was still out there in this world somewhere?

Logan's face shot through her mind and she ducked onto a chair with weak knees. Her gut cramped and her skin was suddenly clammy and heated, unlike anything she'd ever felt in her life.

Love? Really? With a woman she couldn't stand? No way. What were the odds of that? Love blossomed after you got to know someone, or fell hopelessly in love at first sight. She wasn't stupid; she knew it could happen either way.

But with Logan? She almost snickered as she massaged her stomach. Surely it didn't happen if you hated everything about someone, even if you still wanted to fuck them recklessly. That was just lust. Right? Yes, yes, it was. Lust could be overbearing, make you confused and out of control. Lust. That's what it was. But it was over, and thankfully, long gone.

Her mother cleared her throat. Bree turned to look at her just as her mother covered the mouthpiece. "I saw that. Sweet pain of love has a very nice hue around you. Feels good, huh?"

Bree narrowed her eyes. Jesus, could her mom be right? Wasn't she always right? Could she be in love with the woman she wanted to bash over the head with a "get with the real world" stick, then delve her fingers palm deep inside?

No fucking way. She shook her head and smiled as her mom waved her hand in disapproval.

Could she have fallen in love without ever knowing it? With Logan Delaney of all people?

The thought seemed impossible, yet the butterflies awakening in her stomach told a different story. Bree closed her eyes while she assimilated this revelation. Unbelievably, the woman she hated, even despised for her loose morals, may actually be the one—her soul mate.

Chapter Eleven

Logan stepped back and stared in stunned disbelief as the black-and-white photo shuttled out the end of the printing press.

A solid month of sweat and blood, nibbling on the barest of food, and napping only when her body demanded rest, and the reward was staring her in the face.

With her heart fluttering in her chest, she removed the sheaf from the chute and studied her creation. The photograph was perfect, every angle visible, but would the words be inside the faces?

She rushed to the desk and drew a magnifying glass from the drawer, then pulled the light closer to shine over the paper. There, in tiny little letters, was the article her grandfather had written to accompany her grandmother's photograph, or vice versa. She could read every word clear as day, and with a little more tinkering, she might be able to make the letters clearer so they could be read by the naked eye.

With a sob, she sank into the desk chair. She'd done it! She'd accomplished what she set out to do almost from the second she saved this building from the auction block, spending the last cent of her inheritance to preserve their legacy for the future. If only she hadn't let her needs overpower her dreams, this could have been done years ago. She knew as soon as the last thought scurried through her mind, it wouldn't have meant as much then as it did right this very second.

Her first instinct was to call her agent, the very person who begged her to give up all this nonsense and focus on her artwork for the rich and famous clients who continued to multiply as word spread of the services she offered alongside the artwork. Logan automatically reached for the phone then with a shake of her head slowly withdrew her hand. Dialing her number wouldn't do her any good today. Darla was still pissed at Logan for turning down the job of a lifetime—an all expenses paid trip to the beaches of Cancun, and a special, high-class client who'd requested Logan by name. For the past week, she could have been tanning, and fucking, and getting paid handsomely to paint the mystery woman's body. And yet, she'd turned it down without a qualm; the job hadn't sparked a single twitch of desire in her.

She hadn't cared, not then, or now, the money suddenly unimportant. Hell, in the last ten days, she'd turned Penny away twice. The callous bitch had become a pain in the ass with her constant demands. She had more than enough artwork displaying her perfect, artificially enhanced tits, so what the hell could she possibly want with another painting this quickly? Logan shook her head to dismiss the question as irrelevant. Penny wasn't after any canvas. She was after sex. She wanted Logan to scratch the itch that she couldn't get relieved anywhere else. And, just like a drug addict who needed a regular fix, she'd become totally dependent on Logan to supply the sex she craved on demand. Well, not anymore. Penny, together with all the other sad individuals who beat a path to her door, could go fuck themselves for all she cared.

Logan leaned back in her chair and smiled at the photograph, pushing away the thoughts that only caused her discomfort. Bree had opened the door to this moment with her outburst and accusations. Since then she had been to hell and back to find a way to prove her wrong. And now she had, and she wanted nothing more than to share this wonderful outcome with Bree.

Would she be proud of her achievement? Or would she snub her nose? Either way, Logan wanted to know, wanted Bree to see she could do it, that she had done it, that she'd waved away her sick daily life, and all the sex that entailed, to show Bree she wasn't a coward, that she could change and be worthy of her respect.

Somehow, Logan had a feeling that she'd be proud.

She hadn't heard from or seen Bree since their fight. A couple of times when frustration robbed her of sleep she'd almost dialed her number, desperate for any crumb of comfort, even just to hear her voice on the answering machine, but fear of rejection prevented her from doing so.

Now it was probably too late.

Or was it?

With confusion clouding her mind, she reached for her cell.

If anyone would know what she should do, Paula would. She always had a way of knocking Logan back on track. And right now, she desperately needed her ear, and her shoulder.

❖

Bree was nearly back to business as usual. She couldn't count the number of clients she'd flipped in the past month.

Hell, she'd given up count. She couldn't concentrate on anything other than searching, and finding, love for everyone else. She didn't have a choice…it was the only thing that kept her mind off Logan. The days and nights were all a blur, folding into one another like cream dissolving into coffee.

As sick as the notion was, she was almost bored with the daily routine. She spent her whole life searching for love matches for strangers. She arranged meetings and interviews, pandered to their every need, and no matter what she did or where she went, Logan was still right there—in her thoughts, in her dreams, everywhere. She didn't know how, but there she was, like a non-stop movie playing in her head twenty-four seven.

Bree pushed away from her monitor with the aquarium fish scrolling across the screen, and opened the filing cabinet. Might as well get her day started since staring into space, and into her visions, was too painful to bear.

She glanced over her shoulder as Sienne stomped into the room and tossed a folder on her desk. "This woman will not stop calling. I told her we were booked solid this week, but she insists you told her you would work her in." She pumped her fists on her hips. "Can you please take care of this before I say something mean and nasty to her?"

Bree nodded and turned back to thumb through the files in search of the client she was due to have lunch with today at noon. "I'll take care of it."

Sienne sighed. "Yeah, okay."

Bree imagined her rolling her eyes but didn't look around. "I said I'll take care of it, Sienne, and I will, promise."

"Mmm hmm. Just like you're taking care of the meeting you have in five minutes in the coffee shop around the corner."

Bree whipped around. "Fuck! I forgot." She grabbed her Styrofoam coffee cup and downed the contents then grabbed her purse and dodged out of the office. She'd hardly gone five paces before she remembered she'd left her BlackBerry on the desk. When she raced back into the office, Sienne held out the cell phone, a knowing expression tattooed on her face. Bree pursed her lips then started for the front door once again, when she realized the client's file was also still lying on her desk. She stopped, expelled a deep breath, and slowly turned around again. Sienne was there, holding out the file, shaking her head and giving Bree that exasperated look that seemed a permanent feature on her face these days.

"Why don't you take a day off and get your shit together?"

"My shit is together."

"Yeah? You could have fooled me. You're about as together as chalk and cheese."

Bree grinned and shook her head. Sienne knew her too well to be fooled. Hot air smacked her in the face like a wet dishtowel the second she pushed open the glass doors and stepped outside. Thankfully, the coffee shop was only a few steps away.

Truth was, she didn't have her shit together and she hadn't in only God knew how long. It had been a month since she walked away from Logan with her pussy scalding hot. She couldn't rip the bitch out of her mind no matter how hard she tried. It was affecting her business, her daily life, her much needed sleep, and was making a mockery of her emotions. Images scrolling behind her lids faster and faster every night were controlling her, and she hated that more than anything—losing control. She'd never lost it to another living soul, and here she'd gone and practically shoved it in the hands of that whoring, sexy bitch.

Quickly, she made her way down the sidewalk, her high-heel pumps tapping against the concrete with her hurried steps. Maybe Sienne was right, a few days to herself might not be such a bad idea. Lord knew she was useless around the office lately, though she'd flipped the clients much faster while trying to wipe the kissing bandit from her mind.

No. She shook her head. She couldn't take time off. Her clients needed her, depended on her, and if nothing else, it was a daily reminder of what she wanted, and didn't want, in her life, in her future.

Furthermore, this sexual craving could have been remedied had she not been so hasty in forcing the break with Natalie. So what if there wasn't love? There was sex, and lots of it. Very satisfying safe and routine sex, but dammit, it was still sex, and it was still satisfaction.

With a growl, she knew her thoughts were all wrong. She'd done the right thing, this she knew. It wasn't in her nature to cheat, and cheating is exactly what she was doing—would have done—if not physically then in her mind. That safety net of things that were never meant to be was only furthering the inevitable. She and Natalie weren't meant to be together and she prided herself for finally seeing their relationship for what it truly was—loveless.

Love. She almost snickered at the word as her heels punctuated her thoughts. Worse, she'd felt that love, or the possibility of it, with Logan. How could that be? She barely knew Logan, and what she did know, wasn't good. She fucked her clients. She was nothing more than an artistic hooker, a call girl who offered her body and her art in return for vast amounts of money. So why was she still here, ripping through her thoughts, through her heart, daily? A woman like her shouldn't have the power to turn Bree's world upside down, let alone dominate her mind. But she had. Somehow, she had.

When someone bumped into her, Bree jerked around and stared straight into her tormentor's eyes. *Logan.*

Her stomach did several somersaults before she focused and held her head high. "Excuse me, I have a meeting." She scooted around that sexy body but was roughly jerked back by a firm grip around her wrist.

"Talk to me, dammit." Logan's eyes pleaded as Bree looked up into them.

"We don't have anything to talk about." Bree glanced down at the fingers wrapped around her flesh. "Let go of me."

Logan took a step toward Bree, her grip loosening, but not letting go. She crooked a finger under Bree's chin and lifted her face. "I have to show you something."

Bree shook her head when she knew she should knee the bitch and run for her life. Those eyes pinned her down like a thumbtack on a pegboard. "Get your damn hands off me, Logan."

"Kiss me."

"Fuck you."

"God, I want to do that, too, but right now, I want to kiss you." Logan turned and dragged Bree with her, leading them into the alley between the coffee shop and the bookstore. She didn't stop until she was deep into the crevices between two Dumpsters.

Bree resisted, but not nearly as much as she could have, not near what she knew she should do. Dammit, she wanted Logan, wanted Logan chasing her, seducing her.

Logan spun around and pressed Bree against the brick wall and her mouth was hot against her lips before she ever knew it was coming. Her tongue snaked between Bree's teeth, slipping easily inside, and Bree felt herself moan.

Then Logan moaned with her, pressing her hips against Bree, circling in demanding thrusts.

Bree gave in, and kissed her back, her fingers sliding through the soft strands of her hair, pulling her closer, needing her closer.

Logan didn't stop kissing her, kept delving her tongue deep, and grinding herself against Bree in quick pumps.

Bree hooked a leg over Logan's hip and met her harsh rhythm, her orgasm already scattering to the edge. What the hell was she doing? She was about to make out with a woman she despised, and in public, for crying out loud, and she was loving it, and wanting more.

Logan lifted her and Bree locked her heels around her back, driving herself against that firm, tight stomach.

"I need you, Bree. I want you so bad." Logan wedged a hand between them and shoved against Bree's enflamed pussy.

Bree let out a soft cry and pumped harder and faster, desperate to come by Logan's hands raping her mind. She held on tighter, rocking against her hand. "I need to come, Logan. Please, just make me come."

Logan let loose her formed hold around Bree's crotch and ripped at the clasp of her slacks. Bree unlocked her death hold and put her feet against the ground, longing for the feel of Logan's flesh buried inside her.

A door slammed somewhere from the alley and Bree jolted out of her trance. She blinked and shoved Logan back, realization slamming through her mind with lightning speed.

Tears stung her lids as Logan stared at her with desperate

eyes. "Stay away from me, Logan. Far, far, away." She took a step away, her heart already dragging, her pussy throbbing with much needed attention, unable to tear her gaze off Logan's gorgeous face. "Please."

Logan's eyes dropped and she looked pained by Bree's plea. When she looked back up, Bree almost flung herself back into her arms. God, was she acting? Could she really be that torn about this ridiculous predicament they'd somehow woven themselves into?

"Here. I wanted you to see this." Logan thrust a piece of paper toward Bree, but Bree shook her head.

"I can't do this anymore. Please, I'm begging you, stay away from me." Bree turned and pounded down the alleyway, her heart damaged, her ego bruised, and her body steamy with need.

Logan wasn't right for her, no matter how bad she wanted her. Heaven help her, she didn't understand a bit of this conflict, but her pussy throbbing was proof she was neck deep in it, whatever it was. Somehow, she had to put Logan out of her mind once and for all. She was bad for Bree. Very bad.

She all but raced into the air-conditioned coffee shop, daring a glance over her shoulder to see if Logan was behind her.

God, she wanted her to be there, wanted her hot on her heels, chasing, pursuing. When she didn't find the woman she desperately wanted to be there, she turned to her surroundings in search of her client.

The clock above the counter proved she was slipping. For the first time in her life, Bree was late for a meeting.

Fuck. She'd never been late for anything in her life.

She found her client, Maddie, staring uneasily at her

so she marched across the room, willing her heart to stop slamming against her ribs, and slipped into the booth opposite her.

When the waitress approached, she ordered an iced latte and composed herself with a few steady breaths.

"You okay?" Maddie asked.

"Yep, just running behind this morning." Bree looked out the window, but Logan was nowhere to be seen, thankfully… unfortunately.

What had she wanted? And what was she trying to show Bree? For crying out loud, it didn't matter. She didn't want anything to do with the bitch, right? Fuck. She did. She wanted to kiss her again, wanted those strong hands roaming over every inch of her, making her come and scream.

She pressed the images to the back of her mind to concentrate while she listened to Maddie detail her requirements. Something crept along her consciousness and she struggled for clarity. Maddie was talking yet Bree couldn't concentrate on those valuable details. Her words were important—Bree needed those details to make Maddie happy, to fulfill her obligation. Realization slammed hard. Oh shit, she was tired of this, of listening to the boring details of people groveling for someone else to find what they were too fucking lazy to go out and find themselves.

Bree almost gasped at her thoughts. She loved her job, adored finding what no one had been able to find—their true loves. Right? Yes. She did, and she always would.

Logan! The bitch was fucking with her mind. She had to get it back together, somehow, someway, she had to get this nonsense out of her mind and step back on her chosen path of life.

So she studied Maddie. She was very easy on the eyes,

and very confident. She possessed an air of independence that Bree liked in women. And she resembled Natalie, not only in the cap of dark hair that framed her heart-shaped face but in her attitude toward a potential relationship.

Suddenly, she wondered if Logan would seduce a woman like Maddie. Would she have already convinced her to leave, to go home with her, to fuck her? Wasn't that the type of person Logan was? A player?

Of course she was, and Bree knew Maddie would have already succumbed to Logan's charm, would probably already be screaming by her hands.

The thought sent anger boiling over. What the fuck was Logan doing to her?

For a brief moment, Bree was tempted to proposition Maddie, exactly like she figured Logan would do it. A quickie fuck with someone like Maddie would solve all her current sexual frustrations, and a no strings, on my terms, loveless arrangement was better than no sex at all.

Oh God! Bree froze with the glass of coffee halfway to her lips. What was she thinking? Not only would that reduce her to Logan's base level, but a stupid move like that had the potential to ruin her business if word got out. Her hand shook as she replaced the glass on the table and attempted to pull herself together. She'd just escaped from one loveless relationship and she ought to be looking for love, for that special person, like the majority of her clients, instead of wishing, then not wishing, that she was fucking Logan Delaney.

You found love and let it go.

God almighty, Bree's heart turned somersaults. She'd almost grasped the love she sought. It'd been there. She'd swear on her mother's life that for a few seconds she'd seen it shining bright in Logan's eyes. As mysterious as it was, it'd been there, and it was gone, slipped right through her fingers like grains of sand.

Worse, no matter how many times she etched the impossible in her mind, that nothing could have ever come of her obsession with Logan, the thought of what might have been was tearing her apart from the inside out and there wasn't a damn thing she could do to change the situation.

CHAPTER TWELVE

Logan shifted in the lawn chair and propped her elbows on her knees, watching the crowd weave their way through her paintings—her beloved paintings, even if she'd only admit that to herself.

The day was sunny and warm, perfect for an outdoor art show, the one she'd been coolly convinced was necessary to help boost her real artwork.

Puffy, thick white clouds drifted lazily across the clear blue skies. Logan knew she should be happier than this, but she couldn't be. Everything she was doing, cutting off her old agent and hiring a new one, halting all body paintings, and refusing to speak to anyone who had anything to do with acting, could all be for naught. None of it meant anything unless she could find a way to make Bree give her the time of day again. No, if truth were told, she wanted so much more than to just see her face. She needed Bree like she needed to breathe, as an integral part of her daily life—sharing the good and bad moments as a couple but, most of all, she wanted Bree in her bed. Not that she wasn't there already, in her dreams, the imaginary fucks they shared stemmed from their animalistic pawing were out of this world, impossibly incredible. God, she knew the real thing would blow her fucking mind, and she couldn't think of anything but what it'd be like to hear Bree screaming her name.

She sighed. That wasn't going to happen. Bree had made that clear with tears glimmering in her eyes, pleading with Logan to stay away from her. Bree didn't want her. The sooner she let the idea sink in to her mind, the better off she'd be. Bree had already made it clear, twice, that she wanted no part of Logan. Hell, she wouldn't even take the print, wouldn't even look at it. A simple peek might have been enough to show Bree that her words had struck a chord, and changed Logan.

It didn't help that Bree had clung to her like a life preserver, bucking against her, begging Logan to make her come. Dammit, she wanted Logan. Why wouldn't she admit it? Why was she fighting this with a vengeance?

Logan shook her head. It didn't matter. It was over, and that was just fucking that. She knew it was time, time to ease out of her past and start working toward the future. A future she'd already begun. She smiled and glanced at the moneybox under the table that contained a copy of her signed contract for her grandparents' combined works. The new agent had gone wild over the idea, had gone almost crazy when Logan showed her the photocopy. Life was going to change very soon, all thanks to Bree's truthful, hurtful, outburst.

And the sale of her paintings should give her enough money to put the magazine back in operation, the very dream she'd had all along. That is, if anything sold, and from the looks of the people wandering out the other side of the pop-up tent, she might very well go home with every piece she'd brought, just like the last time. She shook off the downing thoughts. Today she had a new optimism.

She leaned back and searched the faces for any sign of Paula, who'd gone in search of food more than thirty minutes ago. No telling what, or who, had stolen her attention and made her forget her way back to Logan's stand.

In the distance, children's squeals accompanied the rousing music from the merry-go-round and Ferris wheel, and the aroma of cotton candy and boiled peanuts permeated the air.

She reminded herself once again that she was doing this for her own benefit. That selling her artwork had to be done, for that new beginning she desperately needed.

A woman stopped in front of one of her paintings. She glanced over Logan like she was one of the carnies instead of an artist, her nose curling with distaste as she quickly glanced away and moved on to another painting.

Logan angled her head and briefly took in her jeans and tank top. She'd shucked her overshirt within the first hour. Did she really look like an outcast because she chose to wear what was comfortable to her? If so, how had she snagged Bree's attention? Had she felt pity simply because Logan insisted on being who she was?

"Logan Delaney! Oh…my…God! Honey, look, it's Logan Delaney!" Paula screamed from the opposite sidewalk, her mouth agape, one hand thrown to her heart, the other holding a plate of only God knew what delicious food from the many vendors lining the streets. With her was one of their friends, Samantha, who tuned in to Paula's outburst with a knowing smile.

They darted across the blocked-off street, both squealing, and both making a delightful spectacle of themselves.

Logan hung her head and smiled. God, she loved her friends. When the going was getting rough, she could always count on Paula to brighten even the darkest situations, and to slap her back down to size when she was being way out of line.

She hadn't missed a week calling Logan a coward, though her winks proved she was proud of Logan for putting her life on a different path.

Paula skidded to a stop in front of Logan. "Holy Mother of God, it's you—Logan Delaney. It's really you! Do you know how long I've waited to meet you?" Her fake smile faded as she spotted the woman now looking at them over her shoulder. Paula scowled at her. The woman's brow cocked as if she'd missed something important and was trying to catch on. Paula rushed to her, practically nudging the woman into a stumble. "You're not going to buy that, are you?" She pointed to the painting in front of the now wide-eyed woman.

Samantha winked at Logan then sidled up to Paula, giving the woman an apologetic smile. "Darling, we already have one very similar to that one, remember? Leave this poor woman alone so she can finish her shopping. She, too, is eager to have one of these priceless pieces." Samantha cooed and pulled at Paula, notching up her polite English.

"I don't care! It's not by *Logan Delaney*. I want them all! Do you hear me? All…of…them!" Paula stamped her tennis shoe against the pavement like a scorned teenager, her mouth dragging into a frown.

Logan stood, too amused by the show to sit a second longer. She went to Paula and held out her hand. "It's a pleasure to meet you."

Paula shoved her plate in Samantha's grasp and took Logan's hand in both of hers like a priest giving a blessing. "Oh no, the pleasure is all mine. Really." She curtseyed then leaned forward and kissed the back of Logan's hand.

Logan jerked her hand away and growled under her breath. "Do that again and I'll sew your pussy shut."

Paula grinned as she straightened to her full height and winked. “How much?”

“Excuse me?” Logan glanced over her shoulder and almost snickered as the “nose to the sky” woman wedged closer to the painting with Paula’s distraction.

Three people had eased under the tent from the left, and a couple holding hands had stopped at the front, all eagerly checking out her artwork.

Logan’s heart did a jolt. Paula’s little show had worked.

“For everything. I want everything!” Paula dragged her tote bag off her shoulder and dug inside. “I’ll write you a check right now. Name your price!”

“Not this one.” The first woman had cash in her hand, waving it around like a flag.

“And we’d like this one,” another couple said.

“Do you have a card? I’d love this one in a different color,” a single woman, who’d somehow snuck in without being noticed, announced from behind Logan.

Paula gave the crowd a glare then looked back to Logan with a sheepish grin. She winked. “Looks like I’ll be needing a card as well since these *vultures* are going to snag your beautiful pieces.”

Logan wanted to hug her. God, how she loved this woman. Who could ask for a better best friend?

The next few hours swarmed into a complete haze. She answered questions, gave out business cards from eager people, boxed up paintings for buyers, and smiled. God, she’d never smiled so much in her life, well, not in the past few months, anyway. The very pit of her soul had been painted into every artwork, and people were buying them, loving them, and asking for more.

Finally, the crowd slimmed and she dropped into the chair, her heart swelled with the many compliments she'd received, and her mind racing with the many appointments she'd set up for possible new clients, for real people who cared about her and her artwork.

She was scanning the few faces left on the blocked streets when an older woman stopped in front of her tent, straight silver hair tucked behind her ears, and cocked her head to the side.

Logan resisted turning away, but the woman's eyes held her rooted to the chair. God, they looked familiar, like she'd looked right into them before, though she couldn't place who or where.

She couldn't look away from the woman as she darted in front of a couple who gave her a brief glare for cutting them off before continuing. The woman approached, her expression quizzical, scanning Logan's face like she knew her, like she was memorizing her.

Logan rose from her chair, suddenly nervous, and puzzled by the woman's strange behavior.

"You're in love, though you don't know it…but sad, and angry." The woman glanced down at the last two paintings sitting against the easels before looking back at Logan. "You think you've lost her."

Logan widened her eyes, now definitely concerned. It wasn't in her nature to be rude to people who acted a little out of their mind, but she wasn't opposed to showing her ass if need be, either. She quickly glanced around, more at ease to see two groups of people passing her tent, and a couple holding hands who'd stopped to scan one of her pieces.

"Trust me, I'm not a psycho. And it's not over. You haven't lost her…yet," the woman said, her firm expression daring Logan to challenge her theory of something she couldn't possibly know.

Logan cocked a brow, wondering if she'd said her thoughts about people being crazy out loud. She knew she hadn't. "I'm sorry, do I know you?"

"No, I'm afraid we've never met. Well, not in person anyway. Seems your aura matches someone else I know."

"My what?" Logan knew she should walk away, but she was too engrossed in the weird conversation not to play along. She chuckled. "Aura? I thought those were invisible."

"Not to me, they're not…and yours is blinding."

"Wow. Really? Does it match my bright paintings?" Logan playfully looked down at her jeans. "Maybe it's the hues of paint I use, confusing people who can see auras?" She shrugged and smiled but quickly saw the woman was dead serious when she didn't share the humor.

"I see why she likes you." The woman grinned and a dimple formed in the corner of her mouth. "You're a smartass. I like that."

Logan nodded, knowing for sure this woman had a screw loose. "Yeah, well, I do try."

The woman stepped in front of one of the paintings and pointed. "This one…how much?"

Logan hesitantly moved around to the front of the painting and her heart dropped. How had she missed this very painting after walking through them all day? She stammered. "Um, that wasn't supposed to, I mean, it's not for sale. I was using it as a prop." Logan lied. She'd never meant to bring this particular piece at all. Paula must have accidentally crated it along with the other paintings. Dammit, she should have been watching more carefully.

"Hmmm, your aura changed. And your cheeks are

flushed." The woman smiled. "She loved this one, didn't she?"

Logan took a step back, not close to liking anything this woman had to say anymore. Her words were eerie, and excessively close for comfort. There was no way a total stranger could know this much about her.

Fuck! It was true. Bree had loved it, and Logan wanted to salvage whatever fragment of memories she could for as long as she could. It might seem stupid to some, but for some reason, this orange and purple artwork was her last connection to Bree—something to remind her of Bree every time she passed it.

Logan chuckled and hung her head for a second. "Lady, I don't know who you are, or how…" She glanced back down at the painting. What good would it do her to hold on to it? Nothing. And she knew it. Bree had gone from her life, had begged to be gone, and God knew Logan wanted to change that, but the fact still remained, anything she could have had with Brianna Hendricks was over, over long before it ever had a chance to begin and this painting wasn't going to make the slightest difference to her future now. With her head held high, she faced the woman once again. "I've changed my mind. The painting is for sale."

"Splendid!" The woman swung her purse around and dug inside. "This will make my daughter very happy. She loves vibrant, bright colors." She smiled and withdrew her checkbook. She began writing while Logan slowly withdrew the painting from the stand. Her throat tightened as she opened the end of the cardboard box. With a final glance at something Bree actually seemed to love, Logan lowered the artwork into the container.

It was time to kiss the what-ifs good-bye. Time to direct

her attention toward the future; no more brooding about what probably could have never been.

When she turned back, fighting back the lump attempting to choke her, the woman held out the check. Logan resisted telling her she hadn't named her price, but she couldn't. Whatever price was on the check didn't matter. It was a check she knew she'd never cash.

She just about managed a professional smile as she handed the woman the box and took the check from her grasp. "I hope your daughter enjoys it." *I hope she loves it half as much as I loved watching Bree's expression the first time she saw it, how she made me think my soul on canvas was priceless.*

The woman patted Logan's hand, and something sparked with the touch. "She will, sweetie, she will. This will open her eyes, for sure."

Logan had the urge to crawl into the woman's arms and cry, to let this woman smooth down her hair and shush away her tears. God, what was wrong with her? She'd never been a sap a day in her life.

She shook her head to wipe away the uncharacteristic thoughts.

The woman gave her a concerned stare then turned and started down the street. The crowd had thickened once again.

Logan watched the top of the woman's head, taking away the last link she had to a woman she couldn't tear from her mind. When the woman was out of sight, swallowed in the thickness of late-afternoon strollers, Logan looked down at the paper, which wasn't a check at all, but a rectanglular sheet from a notepad.

A single message was written across the center.

Love is priceless.

Logan jerked back around and struggled to find her, but there was no sign of silver hair. Her heart scampered against her ribs and she could barely breathe as she desperately searched for the stranger.

Dammit, she'd just given away the last shard of Bree. Of love.

She took a step into the street, but there was no sign of her.

"Hey, Ms. High and Mighty Artist, you ready for that celebration dinner?" Paula snapped Logan from her trance. When Logan didn't immediately respond, Paula followed her gaze. "What is it?"

Logan shook her head. "Nothing." She turned back to the almost empty tent. "Let's get this show packed up."

Paula turned around. "Oh yeah, what, you want to take the concrete home with you? There's only one painting left, which you're going to give me because you love me so much." She gave Logan a joker smile.

Logan managed a grin when her heart was aching. "Deal. And I owe you a drink for that little show. You're amazing." She folded an empty easel and propped it against the table.

"Amazing? Really? Don't recall ever being called amazing when sex wasn't involved." Paula followed suit and started folding easels. "I think I should get two drinks for that accomplishment."

Logan laughed, and though it felt real, it wasn't. She wasn't sure anything would be real from this day forward. She'd lost love, and Bree, and met a woman who'd read something in her that shouldn't be known to another living soul. Yet the stranger had known Logan, and knew her heart was a tangled mess, something she'd been hiding from everyone.

"Two it is."

"Cool. And then you can tell me who, or what, put a frown on your face today after this magnificent turnout."

"I guess I'm just feeling a bit numb at the speed this all took off. Like all this is a dream from which I'll wake up disappointed," Logan lied.

She didn't want to share what was in her mind, what was lacking from her heart. Those things needed to stay sheltered for now, and the less she talked about them, the longer she could keep from falling apart. God knew, she wasn't too far from stepping into the dark abyss, a place she'd never been in her life.

Dammit, she'd missed her chance, and might never have it again.

CHAPTER THIRTEEN

Three hours later, Logan pulled herself onto a barstool at their favorite nightclub, ready to drink herself into oblivion, anything to drive Bree, once and for all, from her mind.

Logan inwardly smiled at the thought. There was no drinking the matchmaker away. Bree's sexy image had embedded itself too deeply in her mind, and seemed to be stuck there for the long haul.

With the thundering rock music blaring from the speakers, Logan sighed and resigned herself to the fact that everything would be okay. Even if she never saw her again, life would move forward, and she was a better person for having known her, for having kissed her, for having almost fucked her.

The days ahead of her would make her the woman she'd wanted to be all along, and she was proud of herself for her achievements, even if they took her much longer than necessary.

Paula waved her hand for the bartender and swiveled the stool around to face Logan. "What's your pleasure, pouty face? Shot of vodka, whiskey…a whole fucking bottle of each?" She grinned and turned to face Vanessa, the owner, who doubled as bartender for the crowded Saturday nights. Although not tall, she dominated the bar with her Goth makeup and short, straight black hair that glimmered blue beneath the arc of strobe lights.

"What'll it be, sexy?" Vanessa winked at Paula, her dark brown eyes almost black in the dimly lit room.

Paula leaned forward until she was nose-to-nose with Vanessa, who didn't bat an eye at having her personal space invaded. "You, spread eagle, on this bar top."

Vanessa slicked her tongue out and ran it across Paula's lower lip. "You couldn't handle me, spitfire. I growl and bite like hell, and mark the shit out of my territory." Vanessa chomped her teeth together.

"Ouch…don't tease me, witch." Paula backed away and slapped a twenty on the counter. "Logan here needs a celebratory bottle of vodka. As of today she's San Fran's hottest new artist." She clapped Logan on the back.

Vanessa took the money and turned toward Logan. "Weren't you that already? God knows you've left a trail of broken hearts all across this city." She winked with thickened black lashes and moved away from the counter only to return within seconds with a bottle of Absolut.

"Go easy on the shots…and the women." Vanessa set three shot glasses on the counter and moved to another patron.

"The parking around here is fucking ridiculous." Samantha sidled up to the bar between Logan and Paula and sighed. She glanced at the bottle and then the glasses. With a grunt, she picked up the bottle and turned her back to the padded edge of the counter. She hung an arm over each of them. "Okay, ladies, tonight we're going to get drunk as shit, and tomorrow we're going to regret every sip while sucking down BC Powder and nursing hellacious hangovers. God, don't you just love life?"

They all laughed, no doubt remembering the effects of their nights out, how reckless they could be with a designated driver. Sam led the way to a table near the dance floor, where the crowd was always thick with onlookers.

Logan swung a chair around and straddled it, looking over the dancers. She recognized several women, most of whom had a notch in her bedpost, although there were a few new faces and some she hadn't had the pleasure of getting around to yet.

Why, suddenly, did she have no desire to seduce one home to her bed? Wasn't she going to forget tonight? Wasn't she going to drink away all those erotic images from her mind and make a fresh start?

Wouldn't taking someone home be falling right back into the old game she'd vowed to leave behind?

Sam scooted her chair back and pointed toward the poolroom. "That one wants to fuck you right here, Logan. Can't you feel her undressing you right now, slipping her hands into those tighty-whites to finger fuck you?"

Logan flicked the briefest of glances to the sexy blonde leaned against the doorjamb, one of her booted feet kicked back against the wall, holding the cue stick against her body in a seductive pose, then quickly turned away, resisting the urge to look again at the gorgeous woman watching her. She took a sip from the glass Paula handed her then grinned at Sam. "Not every woman in this bar is here to fuck someone like you, you sex maniac."

Sam downed her shot and slammed the glass onto the table. "You're right, not every woman is, but that one sure is, and she's got her sights trained on you, baby." She tapped her empty glass and looked at Paula with her eyebrow raised, telling her she was ready for another.

"Damn, you're a bottomless pit." Paula groaned and poured two more shots. She looked toward the poolroom and spotted the woman in question. "Hot damn. If you don't do her, I sure as hell will."

Logan shrugged and turned up her glass. The liquor burned a delightful path down her throat, heating her nerves within seconds. "Have at it."

Sam gave her a quizzical stare and looked over her shoulder at Paula. "Am I hearing this right? Did she just toss her sloppy leftovers in your lap?" She turned back to Logan. "What's up with this shit? You sell a bunch of damn paintings, thanks to me and my sidekick over here, and now you're too good for the free pussy in this bar?"

Paula chuckled then gave a flirty wink to a woman cutting around their table. Logan followed her gaze. The woman's skirt was hiked up her leg, showing way more skin than should be allowed without her standing on a corner.

Logan almost cringed with her mental statement. Hell, she used to carry women home dressed just like her and it didn't matter what they were wearing, the clothes were normally shed within minutes of slamming the door behind her.

She took a look around and noticed most of the women were dressed identically, almost like a uniform, showing as much cleavage as humanly possible without being X-rated, carrying their drink of choice, and all of them, without exception, wore a fuck me smile on their faces.

Had she really found them sexy? Or appealing? Why?

With a sigh, she shook off the thoughts. Today's adventure had marked her somehow. Tomorrow would be different. She'd wake up in the arms of a stranger, she wouldn't know her name, and she wouldn't care, and then life would continue, just like that. Simple.

"Truth or dare," Sam announced and spun her chair around to face the table.

Logan turned to look at her, already seeing the mischievous grin spreading across Paula's face. Their little game had landed them more fucks than either of them could count. God, they were pigs, plucking women from these very surroundings, taking them home to fuck all night, then shooing them away come morning light, all on a dare.

Had she been that kind of person? With Sam's watchful eyes, she knew she had.

Suddenly, Logan wasn't in the mood to play. "Truth."

"Pussy!" Samantha downed another shot and instantly set her glass in front of Paula with another impatient tap-tap. "Hurry, fill me up so I can tolerate her for the next few hours. She's out of her mind stupid tonight."

Logan grinned and crossed her arms across the top of the chair. "Truth."

Sam rolled her eyes and sank back against her chair. "You're killing me! What's happened to my Logan, the player?"

"She's waiting for Samantha to get her thumb out of her ass so she can ask the question." Paula slid the shot glass across the table and Logan grabbed it just before it reached the edge. She downed the contents with a hiss as the fire scorched her mouth and throat.

"Fine! Pussy." Sam leaned forward. "When was the first time—"

"Hold up! I got this one." Paula scanned Logan's face and then cocked her head. "Why are you being such a coward? Why don't you call her?"

Logan squinted, then glared before she looked away.

The strobe lights pulsed around the room, highlighting the dancers wedged against each other, their bodies grinding to the sensual beat.

"Ooh, someone hit a sore spot. Do tell." Sam grabbed the bottle, refilled the glass, then nudged Logan's arm. "Here, drink this first. I want the juicy stuff, like, who we're talking about."

"No one." Logan downed the shot and attempted to steer her away from this topic before it had time to take root.

"Brianna Hendricks," Paula said.

"Shut up." Logan ground her teeth and gave Paula a glare.

"The matchmaker? Bree Hendricks?" Sam looked between Logan and Paula. "Stop glaring at each other and fucking tell me."

"Logan here has a crush on her."

Logan shook her head and looked toward the poolroom doorway. The blonde was angled over the table, a luscious ass filling out a pair of Levi's very sweetly. She looked up before her shot and trapped Logan in her sights. Her eyes told Logan she wanted alone time with her, told her what she'd do with her in that time, what she wanted Logan to do to her.

Logan looked away and refilled the glass, downed the contents then refilled it again. "I don't have a damn crush."

"Yes, you do. You've been pining over her for months now."

"Brianna Hendricks…seriously?" Sam cocked her foot into the chair and sighed. "Well, you sure know how to pick 'em. Sweetie, you know she has like a fucking famous lawyer girlfriend, right? Been together for like a year or something. I'm talking major bigwig butch who's feisty as hell in a courtroom. Natalie something or another."

Logan snapped around to face Sam. She'd heard that name before. Where? From Bree? No. She would have remembered a woman's name rolling off that tongue. Not Bree.

While concentrating hard on when and where she'd heard that name, she refilled her glass twice more, searching the deepest part of her memory for a clue.

In the coat closet, Bree's assistant had interrupted their kiss, to announce Natalie had landed and they were still on for the night.

Motherfucker, the bitch had a goddamn girlfriend. She'd had one the whole time Logan was making an ass out of herself trying to seduce her. Fuck if she hadn't been making a fool out of herself and hadn't even known it.

Logan downed another shot, already feeling woozy from the effects, and resisted clawing at her skin. The odor on Bree that night had been real, and she'd been right. Bree had come straight from one bed, searching for another. Logan's breath caught in her throat along with the lingering aroma of sex and classy perfume that haunted her still.

She glared at Paula, not sure whether to hurl herself across the table and beat her to a pulp, or give her a knuckle shake for finding a way to unveil something Logan had buried deep in her subconscious because she couldn't face the truth. Paula was looking at something over Logan's shoulder. Logan turned to see who had captured her attention and found the blonde smiling down at her like a fucking fairy godmother, sparkling sky blue eyes making all the promises Logan needed.

Lord help her, she was going to fuck up, and she knew it. She was without willpower to refuse such a beautiful invitation, even though no invitation had yet been given. There didn't have to be one; it was written in her eyes.

And right now, she desperately wanted Bree out of her mind, for good.

"Would you dance with me?"

Logan took another shot and rose from her chair. "I'd love to."

The woman took her hand and led her into the thick of the crowd. Sam hooted and catcalled from behind them, though Logan ignored her.

Make me forget, beautiful. Seduce me, please.

Logan wedged herself against the woman then took her arms and draped them around her neck. No use wasting time getting to the point. Tonight, she was going to fuck this woman, and tonight, she would force Bree out of her mind while making someone else come by her hands.

The two-timing bitch didn't deserve a single space in her thoughts. Not anymore.

Logan moved with the beat, leading the dance, seducing, being seduced, until they'd maneuvered themselves into the corner where the large speakers blared and thumped against the floor.

When one song ended and another began, Logan took the woman's hand and led her down the narrow hallway leading to the restrooms and another back room, a place Logan had been many times, where most couples entertained their one-night stands.

Just before she reached the open door, where the hall was the darkest, where the music trembled through the wood paneling, she turned. Before she could talk herself out of what she knew she was about to do, she wedged the woman against the wall and captured her lips, delving her tongue deep inside her mouth, tasting spearmint gum, and inhaling tropical aromas of tequila and pineapple.

The combination was usually arousing, but tonight it

was nauseating. She grabbed the woman's legs and wrapped them around her hips.

The woman's moan resounded like a gun shot in the center of pounding drums, a little offbeat, but unmistakable. Logan circled her hips, grinding mechanically against the blonde's crotch, seeking relief and absolution.

She shut her mind off and released the kiss, trailing a wet path over her cheek and jaw, down her throat, into the vee of her cleavage.

"Oh, God, yes!" the woman panted.

Please fuck me, Logan. I need you inside me. Logan jerked back and stared into the woman's face, knowing the voice inside her head wasn't real, but God, it sure sounded real. The woman's lips were parted and her head was thrown back, caught up in the erotic moment.

Logan looked around, but there was no one there but the two of them. She turned back to the chore, to what would make her forget, and tore at the woman's blouse with her teeth. She needed flesh against her mouth, the woman's nipple hardening against her tongue…she needed to stop, and she knew it. None of this felt remotely right.

It's a long story, and that relationship is now over. Logan gasped and stepped back. The woman wobbled on unsteady legs for a second, then focused on Logan. *Let me explain.*

"I gotta go. I'm sorry." Logan turned and darted from the hallway. She cut a path through the crowded dance floor and beelined for her table. She slapped her hand on the table to break up Sam and Paula's conversation. "Take me home. Now."

Without waiting, she parted a group of women then shoved through the front door. Fresh air impaled her lungs as she sucked in a breath and looked around. The streets were empty save for the cars parked against the curbs and a few patrons standing on the sidewalk for a smoke.

Paula came barreling out behind her. "What the hell was that all about?"

"Nothing. Just take me home, okay?" Logan walked to her truck and waited for her to beep the doors unlocked. She crawled inside and stared out the window, suddenly feeling nauseous.

After a quiet ride home, she finally stumbled up the stairs to her loft, woozy from too many shots of vodka, a few extra to kick out the images of Bree tormenting her mind, the ones that hadn't worked. She kicked off her shoes and listened for Paula's truck to pull away from the curb, no doubt after checking to make sure Logan had locked the door. Paula knew her well.

She shucked out of her overshirt and tank top, then blurrily made her way toward the bedroom but stalled when the vacant walls grabbed her attention.

Empty. Everything looked so empty, matching the way she felt inside. Hollow, and blank, yet determined to forget. Something she couldn't do for the life of her.

One space in particular snagged her attention like a magnet. She made her way to the wall and laid her hand against the vacant space. Bree's hand had been here, right in this very spot, fingering Logan's very soul splattered on canvas.

She let her hand linger, remembering Bree's sweet scent, those eyes telling Logan she wanted more.

With hot tears stinging her eyes, she put her back against the wall and slid down. With her arms dangling over her knees, she hung her head…defeated.

What a moron she was. Bree had come back for her. She may have given up someone else to be with Logan.

And Logan hadn't believed enough. Hadn't trusted Bree or her own instinct. Hadn't believed there might be another innocent explanation for the perfume on Bree's skin. And as for the smell of sex—they'd probably both reeked of sexual pheromones after their phone sex. She had only herself to blame. She'd driven away the one woman she wanted, needed, above all others. And now it was too late to put things right.

But was it too late?

That crazy woman, the one who took the painting, had said some really weird things amongst all that mumbo jumbo about auras. "You think you've lost her" and "you haven't lost her…yet" were two of the statements that had stuck in her mind.

Logan closed her eyes and pictured the woman's face—her eyes, her smile. And suddenly, everything made sense. All the fragments of the jigsaw fell into place. How had she not seen it? The silver haired woman was Bree's mother. Logan's heart jolted in her chest. The woman had bought the painting for her daughter—Bree. She would recognize it and know where her mother got it.

Then what?

What would Bree do? Would she come? Was Logan ready for her?

Dammit, what had she done?

CHAPTER FOURTEEN

What am I doing?

Bree fidgeted in her seat wishing herself anywhere but here while her mother bounced around the room, high on life, and the fact that she'd finally coerced Bree into a blind date after weeks of begging.

She hadn't been on a date with anybody since the disastrous evening with Logan six months previously. The memory of their heated exchange in the restaurant parking lot spooled through her mind in vivid fast moving pictures. They'd gotten so close, so fucking close to doing it right there on the hood of her Lotus.

Maybe if she'd had the courage to go on, and they'd finished what they started, she'd have gotten Logan out of her system. But her innate sense of fairness meant she needed to break with Natalie before committing to Logan, before fucking Logan, and that had been her undoing.

Fuck! Why had she resurrected that particular memory when she was finally getting her life back on track? She hadn't thought about Logan for days. The longing and the pain were fading treacherously slowly. Not nearly fast enough for Bree's self-assurance, but fading, nevertheless.

Here she sat beside a woman she didn't know, and didn't want to know, who'd been smiling like a lunatic from the second her mother escorted her into the house. According to her mother's comprehensive introduction, she was an orthodontist with her own practice, suave in her posture, and gorgeous as hell. And Bree had felt nothing when she shook the woman's hand. Not even a tiny spark of heat, or a fluttering of an irregular heartbeat. She desperately wanted her pussy to clench with eye contact, wanted something to stir in her gut, needed desperately to feel something, Godammit.

Yet, there'd been absolutely nothing and, even an hour later still, there was nothing.

Sure, she possessed everything Bree looked for and wanted in a woman. Dependence, gentlemanly ways, and good looks. The looks were always a must, though she didn't know she'd become so superficial until she'd found herself comparing every woman she passed on the streets to Logan. Yet compared to Logan this woman had nothing Bree wanted at all. Logan had been the one, her soul mate, and she knew it, and it had driven her fucking crazy for months wondering how, or why, when they were so obviously unsuited in every respect.

Bree shook her head to halt the thoughts from imploding her mind once again. No use dwelling on what could never be, and the fact still remained, there never really had been, and never would be, anything with Logan. For a few brief moments, there was something hot and breathless between them, but whatever it was, evaporated like the morning mist long ago and the sooner she nailed that evidence to her mind the better off she'd be.

"Here, sweetie, have a bite of this." Bree's mother all but pushed a dish of ranch dip into her hands and smiled.

Behind those eyes rested determination and something

else, something Bree couldn't read. Her mother was up to something and she couldn't work out what or why, only that she needed to be on her guard.

Bree took the bowl and placed it on the table. "Thanks."

"Don't mention it." Her mother winked and scurried away to another table where a woman and a man chatted quietly.

Love resonated between them. Soft and simple, yet radiantly obvious.

"Can I get you something else to drink?" her date, Toni, asked.

Bree turned around and forced herself to look directly at Toni, not through her like she'd been doing. She was charming, and again, gorgeous, and Bree suddenly wanted to smack that wide smile from her face, to shout from the rafters that she wasn't available or anybody's sex toy, although the woman's eyes said she wanted Bree to be just that—hers.

"No, thank you." Bree turned completely around to face her, determined to give the woman her attention if it was the last thing she did tonight. She owed it to herself and to her mother to give her all, even if her all was only a fraction of what she could have given months ago.

"So, tell me more about yourself." Switching on her business persona, which she used to good effect when extracting information from her clients, Bree picked up a chip and dipped into the cream.

That damn smile widened, if that were possible. Her perfect teeth were almost blinding they were so white, unnaturally white. "I'm a nature girl. I love the outdoors, hiking, sports, camping, and especially the mountains in winter."

Bree mentally shuddered and had to force a smile onto

her face. She wasn't any of those things. She hadn't been camping in a tent since her father, God rest his soul, begged her to at least experience the outdoors, once. Sharing her sleeping bag with critters was not her idea of fun, nor was hiking until her legs quivered, or freezing her socks off on some ice climbing or skiing jaunt. She was a city girl through and through, and curling up on the couch with a movie to watch someone else venture into the wilderness was about as close as she wanted to get to the outdoors.

"How about you?" Toni draped her arm across the back of Bree's chair, already trying to stake her claim on the prize—the prize she wouldn't be getting.

"I'm not an outdoorsy kind of girl, and I hate anything creepy, but I love feeding the pigeons in McLaren Park and sometimes walk barefoot through the grass, though I'm game for just about anything." Bree lied. She had no intentions of doing anything that involved hiking boots or sporty water bottles.

As the thought wove through her mind, Logan flashed in her thoughts. If Logan wanted her to venture into the creepy nights of some wooded terrain, would she go? Yes, dammit, she would. Hell, at this point in time, she'd follow the bitch into the pits of hell and burn for all of eternity just to finish what she wanted so fucking bad to finish.

She wanted to fuck Logan, wanted to be fucked by her, and then, maybe then, she could drive all images from her mind. Right?

Fuck, no. It'd only be the beginning of the end, and she knew it.

"You don't strike me as a person afraid of creepy crawlies." Toni's downcast eyes betrayed her lie.

However, her smile widened once again and she leaned toward Bree. "I bet I could change your mind. Maybe we could take a trip into the mountains one weekend and put it to the test."

Bree grinned and shrugged. "I guess I could be convinced." Not! Especially with this woman. And what was all the fake grinning about? She couldn't even flirt with a woman anymore. She sounded stupid, and she knew it, could hear the miserable attempts.

"You would be, I promise." Toni's fingers trailed across Bree's back, lingering at the nape of her neck, before continuing across her shoulder.

Bree felt the urge to leap from the seat, but controlled the impulse. Only another hour of this self-inflicting bullshit and she could call it a night, and never, ever, allow her mother to con her into matchmaking games again. She should have known better, though she seriously wanted there to be some kind of connection, even if only a sexual one.

Right now, she'd take a hard fuck over the images that were slowly pushing their way back into her mind. Jesus, this was ridiculous, and stupid. It was over, long before it ever began, so what the fuck was her problem? Why couldn't she just walk away from the whole thing without clinging to something that never was?

And here she was again, questioning the same fucked up questions she'd promised herself she'd never ask again.

"Sorry to interrupt, but I wanted to show off my new artwork I've finally had hung," her mother announced from the threshold of the dining room.

She turned and headed into the other room, and the couple sitting closest to Bree and Toni rose from their seats in pursuit.

Bree pushed away from the table, almost too quickly. She needed to get away from this woman, her cool manners, and that damn over-bright smile.

As she followed the previous couple into the room, she could feel Toni hot on her heels, her hand resting on the small of her back like she was already a prized possession. That simple gesture normally made Bree cream her panties, made her yearn for a fuck. Right now, she wanted to turn in the woman's grasp and scream at her, that she was not going to fuck her, or date her, or go tromping in any woods with her, that she wanted her to swipe that stupid smile from her face because it was nauseating. Instead, she stiffened and continued into the room.

Her breath caught and hung in her throat like a thick wedge of cotton wool as she caught sight of the painting tucked beside her mother's oak hutch.

There, in those bright orange and purple hues, was the very painting she'd fallen in love with in Logan's apartment.

Her insides churned, her throat tightened, and her pussy clenched. She wasn't aware she'd gasped until faces turned around, all eyes pinned on her like she was a highlighted exhibit.

Her mother giggled. "I had the very same reaction the first time I saw it, too, dear. It just has that kind of effect on you, like it grabs hold and won't let you go, no matter how *hard* you try."

What was this picture doing here? How had her mother acquired it? What made Logan decide to sell? Bree was so mesmerized by the merging colors that she was unaware that Toni had sidled up to her side until she felt a heavy arm drape across her shoulders.

A sob was trapped in her chest. She could feel it like a heavy weight bearing down on her. She looked to her mother who watched with knowing eyes.

How could she possibly know? How could anyone

possibly know the torment raging through her? But with those glimmering eyes, she knew her mother knew, that she'd known all along.

Her mother nodded then she angled her head, the gesture that silently told Bree it was okay, and that she understood.

"It's amazing," Bree said as she looked back to the painting. "Where'd you get it?"

"At an art show, a few months ago. The artist was selling everything, making a new beginning." Her mother took a loving look at the painting. "I was just biding my time to hang it, for the perfect timing."

Bree narrowed her eyes, looking between her mother and the painting. She shifted to her other foot, fighting the leaden arm tugging her shoulder down, and the need to get answers to questions she had no right to ask.

Toni snuggled into her side as if Bree's movement had beckoned her. She resisted pulling away and allowed Toni to pull her deeper into the crook of her arm. As she stared at the sign that she'd allowed something, love, lust, an incredible need, pass her by, she wished for something more, that she could look up at Toni and want her, want any part of what she had to offer.

It was useless to wish for anything more than the hopeless longing for Logan. Logan was the one, and somehow, some way, Bree had allowed the chance of happiness to glide right through her fingers. Yet even with the notion that she'd been as close to love as she might ever get, she also knew from common sense alone that whatever Logan had to offer, was far less than she was willing to settle for. The lust, the need, the indescribable want, was all a figment of her imagination, and Logan couldn't give her what she truly needed—all of herself.

She suddenly felt utterly alone. Her life, her career, it

was all spent pleasing everyone else but herself. Would it be like that for the rest of her life? With dread, she knew it would be. She wasn't destined to have love for some reason, and the painting, standing like a symbol of her loss against the tan walls, was nothing but a mockery to her personal confession.

Could she live with the way things were? Could she live knowing love was in her past, and might never be in her future?

Toni nudged her and Bree snapped out of her thoughts. She looked up to see that pathetic bright smile and felt her heart jam in her chest.

Whatever she could have with Logan, however small, however miniscule, was more than she'd ever find in the arms of this remarkable woman, and she wanted it desperately.

"Shall we go back to the tables for some dinner?" Her mother moved away from the painting while Bree was held rooted by the bright hypnotic symbol.

There it was, a sign of regret, a sign of what might have been, a sign of what would never be, standing out like a beacon, and Bree willed time to fly by so she could get away, to think, to dwell in her thoughts.

Finally, she looked away and wove her way through the tables, avoiding eye contact with a woman she knew wanted to take her home, to do things to her body she only wanted Logan to do.

Should she? Could she? Wouldn't a night in this woman's arms at least take away the images? Or would it enhance them, make her compare, and need more?

As Toni helped Bree into her seat, she knew a night with her would only infuse the need already thick in her veins, and would be a waste of precious time, no matter how satisfying it could be. Logan, and only Logan, could put out this fire, the same fire ignited in a fucking coat closet. Would it ever go away? Or would she forever want what she never had a chance to have?

When her mother took away her half-empty plate, Bree almost wept. The night was over, and now she'd have to make her excuses and go home—alone.

"You barely nibbled anything on this plate, sweetie. Are you feeling okay?" Her mother stared down at Bree with concerned eyes.

"I just wasn't that hungry." Bree avoided those sympathetic eyes and reached for the napkin. "Besides, you put enough food on my plate to feed half of San Francisco."

"You're always hungry…always." Her mother chuckled. "By the way, what'd you really think about my new painting? The artist was very cute, and just your type of artist—a newbie. Her aura was…like yours."

Bree glanced up at her, the softly spoken words etched with double meaning. How could she possible know? Shit. Her mother always knew. Somehow, she just always knew.

The look suddenly made her angry. Logan was a player, fucking women simply for laughs and giggles. She was not the kind of woman Bree could spend the rest of her life trying to tame. She shook her head, then pushed away from the table. "Her aura couldn't possibly resemble mine, but I wish her much success with her *new beginning*."

Her mother grinned as Bree stepped around the chair. Toni jumped up and stood beside Bree, that sickening smile dominating her face. Jesus, could the woman just fucking stop smiling like a deranged fool? It was almost grotesque, and a total turnoff, though Bree was sure any other woman would have already dragged her out, probably fucked her in the car on the ride home.

She wished for a split second that she found this woman

appealing, that she'd want to fuck her as much as she wanted to fuck Logan, but knew the notion was impossible.

Only one woman could end this torture, and that woman was somewhere in this town, possibly fucking someone else right this very second.

Bree hugged her mother and whispered, "Thanks for tonight. Sorry it didn't work out."

Her mother gave her a squeeze and pressed her mouth against Bree's ear. "It worked out perfectly, exactly the way I planned."

And Bree knew she was telling the truth. Somehow, her mother knew this night would be a fluke, that the woman who was every bit her type, wasn't her type at all, and that tonight would prove to Bree that she was searching in the wrong places all along.

Bree excused herself and allowed Toni to escort her to the car. Now, she had to let her down easy.

"Would you like to go for some coffee?" Toni edged her hip against the car.

"No, but thank you for some great conversation." Bree smiled, knowledge of where she was going when she left here making her heart flutter.

Logan. She was going after Logan. And she was going to fuck her until neither one of them could walk, and when she was done, she was going to drive herself home, and then, and only then, would she have Logan Delaney completely out of her veins.

Toni leaned closer, her face masking something trying to be suave. "I could make the conversation more interesting, if you'd let me."

Bree almost laughed. The woman was pathetic, and desperate. Something devilish took over her mind as she stared at that hilarious Clorox smile. "I appreciate the offer,

Toni, but right now, I have a woman waiting for me across town who I'm going to fuck…all…night…long."

Toni's eyes widened and the smile vanished, finally, from her face.

Bree ducked into the car and revved the motor. Without looking back, she backed out of the driveway, her mind on a one-way streak to hell, and she couldn't wait to get there.

Twenty minutes later, she stared at the oak door of Logan's apartment, willing herself to get out of the car and take that leap of faith. Behind the door, up two flights of stairs, housed the woman she wanted to rip apart. Every image imaginable flitted through her mind as her heart raced.

This was so out of character, totally removed from the sane person she'd claimed herself to be all these years. So what was she doing hanging around outside Logan's apartment like a lovesick teen once again, wanting to burst through those doors and climb those stairs two steps at a time, then fling herself into those strong arms, for nothing more than a one-night fuck? That's all Logan could offer her, and she knew it.

Her stomach churned with renewed tension. She wasn't the sort of person to take the initiative like that. Nor was the person on the third floor the type of woman she'd ever wanted.

And now Logan was everything she wanted, everything she desired. Fuck, how was this possible?

She took a deep breath, willing her heart to settle before it burst through her chest, and opened the door. The night breeze caressed her cheek and whipped through the strands of her hair as she stepped onto the sidewalk and approached the door.

"Just do it," Bree whispered to herself. The words

were anything but calming. In fact, hearing them made her weaker.

With determination, she brushed the hair back from her face and straightened. With one last deep breath, she looked at the buttons lining the right of the door.

A half sob rumbled through her chest as she read the new label for the first floor.

Forever Moments Magazine.

Logan had done it. She'd put her grandparents' love back into operation. Was this the new beginning her mother had talked about? Of course it was, though Bree wasn't sure how she knew, and right now, she didn't care.

She pushed the button for the third floor and heard the buzzer from somewhere above her.

When nothing stirred, she pushed the button once again, now shifting from one foot to the other. Her heart rammed steadily against her chest as she waited, begging her nerves to settle.

When no sounds came, she tried the door handle and was surprised to find it locked. She pushed the buzzer once again and took a step back, staring up to the third floor for any sign of life, terrified Logan would appear behind the window, and another face as well. She didn't think she could stand to be proven a fool tonight.

But nothing appeared in the glass above her, not even a single light. Logan wasn't home. Why would she be? It was Friday and she was probably in the arms of another, on a dance floor somewhere twirling a lover around to some sexy beat.

The thought was unbearable.

Bree turned dejectedly back to her car, feeling foolish, and lacking the common sense her mother raised her to have. With one last glance back at the top floor, she let one last image of Logan fill her mind, and promised herself it would be the last.

It was time to move on, no matter what the future held. She could be proud of Logan from afar, right where she knew she needed to be.

By the time she drove onto her street, she was feeling better, even if she knew the night would bring more virtual images of Logan. She knew it was best this way, no matter how much she'd hoped Logan would have opened that door. It was past time to put this bullshit behind her. Whatever the emotions were, they needed to be put to rest.

With an affirmative smile, she parked the car in the driveway and got out. She beeped the doors locked and looked up into the night sky. The moon was bright, lighting her street and surrounding houses in dull white light.

She closed her eyes for a brief minute and let the breeze calm her, allowed the moment to get her senses back, and to push Logan far into the recesses of her mind. Logan would always be there, but that was okay.

Tomorrow was a new day and she would make the best of it. She always did. It's how she operated. And the next day would be even better, followed by a third. Eventually, Logan would be nothing more than a fond memory.

Bree opened her eyes and stared at the North Star. "Star light, star bright, I beg you for this wish tonight." She mentally wished for happiness and love then blew a kiss to the sky.

"I wonder how many people have wished on that star tonight."

Bree whipped around, automatically taking a step back, and found Logan perched on her front porch steps like a barbarian goddess, her elbows resting on her denim-clad legs, those eyes raking over Bree like unseen, probing fingers.

CHAPTER FIFTEEN

Logan couldn't breathe. For the first time in her life, just the sight of a woman had her frozen, and aroused, yet confused but willing to stand her ground instead of walking away to avoid the whole confrontation. She demanded her body move from its sitting position, for her mind to stop undressing every inch of Bree, and her heart to stop slamming in her chest.

The emotions invading her were incredible, unlike anything she'd ever felt in her life. She wanted to go to Bree, to drag her into her arms and kiss her until she begged for breath. Then she wanted to strip her naked and fuck her until she'd made up for every night they'd been apart, ten, a hundred times over.

But Bree only stood and stared, making Logan wonder what the hell she was doing here, why she ever thought this was a good idea. She suddenly felt totally naked, open, and vulnerable. Did Bree know that she was coming apart one stitch at a time? Could Bree detect from her haggard breathing how frenetically her heart pumped in her chest, or that Logan's body was overheating just from the sight of the gorgeous woman standing immobile in front of her? Did Bree know how bad she wanted her? How her pussy, now flooded with hot juices, pulsed with a need that demanded immediate satisfaction?

Bree seemed to come back to herself. She drew in a sigh, but never moved. "What are you doing here?" Her voice quivered, giving away her emotions, but nothing, no clue to her feelings.

What *was* she doing here? Hadn't she already asked herself that very question over and over while sitting in the dark? To see Bree, to talk to her…to fuck her? Definitely all of the above, and not necessarily in that order.

The pressure of the book in her lap drew her back to the real reason she was here. Her creation, complete and beautifully bound, was why she'd been sitting on Bree's stoop for more than two hours while her imagination ran riot of where Bree had been, who she was with, if she'd fucked, or been fucked. Dammit. She had no right to question Bree's whereabouts, and it was none of her business who she'd been with, or what they might have been doing, but the thought of her in someone else's bed, fucking them, drove her crazy with jealousy.

She mentally shook her head. Bree was here now, alone, and she needed to see the approval in her eyes, to see pride for the mission accomplished. Would she? Or would Bree snub her and send her away, or run like she had in the alley? Would she be thrilled that Logan had spent the last months putting her grandparents' magazine back in operation? That she hadn't had sex since she kissed Bree in that coat closet, that she hadn't wanted to? Except for making love to Bree over and over in her mind, in her dreams, she hadn't wanted to touch any other woman since the night she slammed a stranger against a wall on the night of her art show, and then heard the voice of reason echoing in her head.

She'd changed, all for the better, and hopefully Bree would see that, and accept her.

Ready to face the music, she pushed off the steps and stood. Bree swung her long hair over her shoulder and started down the sidewalk. Every step brought her closer, and every step made fluid pool between Logan's thighs.

Bree was so fucking beautiful, and Logan wanted to fuck her like she wanted to fuck no other, wanted to hear all the sounds she could pluck from her mouth while she made her come.

When Bree stopped in front of her, Logan lost her voice. She held out the book like a peace offering.

Bree stared for several seconds, like she was trying to read Logan's mind, then she took the book, and took another step forward until they were mere inches apart.

Every hair follicle along Logan's arms rose, followed closely by the ones at the nape of her neck. She willed herself to hold still and not to drive herself against Bree for fear of pushing her away.

After what seemed like an eternity of inaction, of palpable tension, Bree rose on her tiptoes and pressed her lips to Logan's. The world tilted on its axis, rocked, and fireworks lit the darkness as her eyelids fluttered shut.

Bree moaned when Logan parted her lips with the tip of her tongue and pulled Bree against her, more harshly than she wanted. She couldn't help it. She wanted this woman so bad pain seared through every fiber of her body.

When Bree draped her arms around Logan's neck, the weight of the book dragging her hand down Logan's back, life felt right once again, better than it ever had. The past months of agony vanished, and the past was nothing more than a memory. Bree was in her arms, with her tongue exploring Logan's mouth, and her fingers splaying through her hair. Sweet Jesus, they were finally going to finish what they started. Bree wasn't getting away again, and from the way she was grinding her hips, Logan knew she wouldn't have to try too hard to keep her close this time.

Bree pulled back, her breaths hard and steady, her eyes demanding closure. "Let's go inside before I rip off your clothes and get us both arrested for indecent exposure."

Logan smiled, content to follow like a puppy on a lead, staying close to Bree, not wanting any distance separating them. Tonight would answer all the questions and maybe, if fate smiled on them, open the doors to their future. A future she hadn't dared to dream might exist until this moment.

Soon, she'd have Bree naked in her arms and she'd know how she looked as well as what she sounded like when she came in person, when Logan's fingers were buried inside her, making her moan and scream from the pleasure.

When Bree closed and locked the door behind them, Logan came apart with sexual desire.

Bree was staring at her, her eyes full of animalistic hunger. With a slow growl, Bree crashed into her, knocking her against the back of the door, clawing at Logan's overshirt while her lips locked on her. She was vaguely aware of the thump as the book hit the floor.

Logan fisted her hand into fragrant locks of curls and dragged Bree's head back. She bent and licked a path from the hollow of her throat up to her jaw, kissing and nipping around her jaw line until her lips rested against Bree's ear, then whispered, "I'm going to fuck you so hard."

Bree swallowed, the movement sending a ripple against Logan's cheek, and gave a helpless cry. "Please, I beg you."

"Oh, you'll beg all right, that, I'm sure of." Using Bree's

hair as reins, Logan twisted her around until her face was flat against the oak door. She wanted to be so gentle, but she couldn't; she'd waited too long. Desire, and need, was her master now, and Bree was her willing slave.

Logan pressed her body against Bree and ground against her ass. She pushed Bree's hair to the side and nipped the curve of her neck, then sucked the skin to ease the sting. "Do you know how bad I've wanted you?"

Bree rolled her hips backward, pushing that splendid ass against Logan. "Show me."

Logan reached around her, grabbed the soft edges of her blouse, and then yanked it open. Buttons flew in all directions, the sound like an exploding firecracker as they ricocheted off the hardwood floor.

Bree sucked in a ragged breath and the action fueled her lust, feeding the animal raging out of control inside Logan. She fanned her hands against Bree's flat stomach, sliding easily against her creamy soft skin until her fingers closed around plump breasts. While her hungry mouth fed on Bree's neck, Logan tore the flimsy scrap of lace that served as a bra apart to expose Bree's nipples to her seeking fingers, then she thumbed the tips while they swelled and hardened into tight buds. Bree squirmed against her, begging with her body to be fucked.

"God, you feel so good in my hands." Logan twirled the jeweled tips between her thumb and index finger, her mind reeling, her emotions overbearing, and her body temperature spiking off the scale.

Nothing had ever felt so right, so perfect, and this perfection was going to kindle the fire all night long, spreading long into the wee hours of the morning. If she was lucky, maybe she could find a way to keep Bree between the sheets all day tomorrow as well. Twenty-four hours wasn't going to be near the amount of time she needed to explore Bree and get this pent up frustration and pain out of her system.

"Logan, please…I need you."

Logan reveled in her panted confession. Bree needed her. She wasn't sure she'd ever been needed in her life. Wanted, sure, but needed? No. If she had been, no one had bothered to tell her, and if they had, she was positive it couldn't feel near as powerful as it did this very second.

She kissed Bree's shoulder. "I'm going to quench that thirst, baby…just hold on a little longer."

Logan released her grip on those tight pebbles and tugged the blouse down Bree's arms, but instead of taking it completely off, she pulled her wrists to the small of her back and hooked the edges into a knot. She knelt, her face level with Bree's rounded ass, and mounded the cheeks into the palms of her hands. "Anyone ever told you what a mighty fine ass you got here?" She bit the covered flesh with a quick nip.

Bree arched back and rolled her hips. "I can't wait. Finish me, Logan. Please!"

Logan smiled and rose, licking a trail along the sexy indention of Bree's spine, until her face was crooked against her cheek. With a slow, easy glide, she caressed a soft line down Bree's back, over the silk slacks covering her ass, and pushed her fingers into the alcove between her thighs.

Bree moaned, rose on her tiptoes, and widened her stance. "Logan, fuck me…I'm on fire."

Logan could feel her heat, her wetness, and she wanted her fingers wedged inside Bree so bad it was making her weak with need. She grabbed Bree's tied wrists and spun her around.

Her chest heaved, pushing out those splendid breasts, her lips parted, and dry.

Logan pressed her mouth against Bree's and sucked her bottom lip between her teeth. "You beg so sweet, Bree. I like hearing you pant, and plead." She cupped Bree's crotch in her hand and pushed against her opening.

When Bree whimpered, Logan dug deeper, practically shoving her panties and slacks into her pussy, almost lifting her off the floor with the thrust.

"Oh, God, please…fuck me, Logan. I need you to fuck me." Bree bucked into her hand, her pussy a heated, sodden, throbbing mound against her palm.

Logan groaned. She'd waited so long for this moment, to hear Bree beg. "Oh, I'm definitely going to fuck you, baby—in my own good time."

Bree drove her hips faster, her head pressed against the door, mewing, and gasping. "I'm gonna come, Logan. Fuck!" She ground her teeth and pressed her head against Logan's shoulder.

Logan slowed her thrusts. "Not so fast, tiger. I need you naked and pumping around my fingers." She withdrew her hand from Bree's warmth and knelt.

Bree groaned. "Hurry, dammit. I can't wait much longer."

Logan looked up at her under hooded lashes, and unsnapped her slacks. She loved seeing Bree like this, desperate, vulnerable. So different from the ice cool "I've got my act together" businesswoman she portrayed to the world. The zipper purred as she lowered it, then with a small tug, the pants fell around her ankles to display a pale pink thong.

She inhaled heat, and sex, her face inches from Bree's

weeping pussy. "Mmmm, you smell so good. I'm going to tease you, and lick you, and take you closer, Bree, and when I think you're ready for me, I'm going to fuck you like you've never been fucked before."

Bree kicked out of her pants, then snapped her black stiletto-heeled pump back down against the hardwood floor with a sharp crack. She circled her hips, staring down over Logan with carnal desire dancing in her eyes. "Put your mouth on me…taste me, Logan. Drive me over the edge."

Fire erupted in Logan's gut with her words. She was so fucking sexy with her legs spread and quivering, her arms tied behind her back, completely at her mercy.

With a smile, Logan hooked her fingers around the thin string looped over her hips, and slid the thong slowly down Bree's legs.

Bree lifted her foot and Logan slipped the underwear off.

She kicked Bree's legs further apart and thumbed her lips apart.

Bree drew in an anticipated breath, and Logan licked the tip of her hood. Bree slung her head back and thrust against Logan's mouth. Sweet. She tasted so sweet, and intoxicating, just like Logan knew she would.

With every swipe of her tongue, Bree mewed like a kitten, making Logan ache.

"Faster, Logan…fuck me with your tongue…I need, relief."

Logan knew how she felt. She'd needed relief for months, thought of nothing but this very moment, how quick, how powerful and explosive it'd be. And now that it was here she just wanted the moment to last forever, wanted to drag out the conclusion for as long as possible.

Her own pussy throbbed with every buck of Bree's slender hips, her inner thighs slick with her own juices.

When Bree's thrusts quickened, Logan knew she didn't have much time. Bree was so fucking close, too fucking close. She had to find a way to slow down the pace.

"Logan, please!" Bree bucked, searching, reaching for the elusive pinnacle of satisfaction.

Logan drew back from her pussy, stalling long enough to blow air across her heated skin, and nibbled her thigh. "Logan, please, what?"

"Don't tease me. I'm so fucking coiled I'll snap."

Logan slicked her tongue out and lightly touched Bree's clit. "I know, I can feel you. You're hot, wet, and almost ready for me." She inserted a finger into her wet opening, circling against her slick walls.

Bree's pussy clenched tight around her fingers. She was so wet. Logan wanted to dive inside her, thrust and pump, until Bree screamed out her release. God, she wanted that so bad, but as much as she wanted this finished, she wanted something else…a new beginning, one that wasn't over too damn quickly either.

Bree rose on her tiptoes, pushing her pussy toward Logan's mouth. "Fuck me, now, with your tongue, I can't wait!"

And neither could Logan. The sounds escaping Bree's lips were too much, and she wanted Bree in her arms, against her bare skin, when she fell over the edge.

She withdrew from the aromatic vee of Bree's thighs, rose, and tugged the shirt off her wrists. Once free, Bree's arms automatically wrapped around her neck, her fingers tangling in Logan's hair.

Logan didn't waste a second capturing those lips. She

lowered Bree onto her back against the cool floor and lay on top of her, wanting to be deep inside her, touching her very soul with the tips of her fingers. Bree bucked against her, soft at first, then wildly grabbing at Logan's clothes.

When Bree locked Logan between her thighs, Logan thrust against her, delving her body harshly against Bree's, sucking in her breath, fire roaring through her body.

The heat was almost unbearable as she pumped into the alcove of Bree's thighs. When Bree tugged at her overshirt, Logan leaned back and allowed her to jerk it off her arms. She tossed it away then reached for Logan once again.

"I'm going to catch fire. I'm so fucking hot, and horny, and…" Bree panted, tugging at Logan's tank top. "Please don't stop, Logan."

Logan smiled with her plea. There wasn't a chance in hell she'd be stopped tonight. Unless a meteor landed on this house, the devil himself couldn't halt her now.

Bree tucked her fingers around Logan's neck and pulled her back down, kissing a wet trail down her throat. She grappled at the tank top. "Get this fucking thing off!"

Logan quickly tugged the tank top over her head and unfastened her jeans. When she looked back down at Bree, desire was packed in those eyes. The expression made Logan gulp.

Bree needed relief, and she needed it now, and Logan was suddenly afraid it wouldn't be enough, that what she had to offer Bree wouldn't be enough. Bree dated prestigious, smart, intelligent women, just like Bree was. Logan wasn't any of those things. She lived in blue jeans, usually darted with paint, and didn't even own a business suit. All she had to offer was sex, her love, her art, and the magazine. She knew beyond a shadow of a doubt she fell way beneath Bree's normal standards.

What in the hell was she doing here with Bree, with those eyes needing and wanting her?

Logan gave a silent prayer she could satisfy her, then leaned back on her heels. It was time to take Bree over the edge, then beg the heavens that Bree would want more, that she'd never tire of wanting, never get enough.

"I'm going to fuck you every way a woman could possibly fuck another." Logan drove against her. "All night long, Bree, you are mine." She leaned down and clamped her lips over Bree's and felt a rush of hot breath feather against her cheeks.

With their tongues circling, matching the rhythm of their hips, Logan soared to a high she'd never encountered. As much as it was terrifying, it was peaceful, fulfilling, and she never wanted this feeling to fade.

She bucked hard against Bree, harder with every thrust, wanting to slow down, then speed up, wanted this over, then beginning again.

Bree wasn't helping with every moan, every thrust, and every tug, telling Logan with her gestures how bad she wanted her, how she wanted all the things rushing through Logan's mind.

Tonight, if only for tonight, Logan was going to make Bree hers.

She needed to smell her, to taste her, to make her come all night. She wanted this night a memory already, wanted the morning light to cascade over their naked bodies, so they could make more memories tomorrow and the next, and, God willing, for years to come.

Logan wedged her hand between their bodies, down, until she found Bree's slick opening. The moisture made her growl, made fluid rush against her briefs, and she snaked the tip of her finger inside. Logan inserted another finger and easily slid inside her. "God, Bree…" Her insides spasmed as Bree tightened around her, grabbing for her, willing Logan to fill her.

Logan sucked Bree's lobe between her teeth, then moved down until her lips rested against the pulse in Bree's neck. She whispered, "I can't be gentle, Bree. I've waited too fucking long."

Before Bree could respond, Logan drilled her middle fingers inside her so hard she practically lifted her off the floor.

Bree cried out and whimpered, her nails clawing at Logan's back.

Logan thrust again, and again, harder and harder with every pump, using her legs for leverage, fucking Bree with her fingers. With every jolt, her own orgasm scrambled to the edge, teetering against the abyss, threatening to take her over without Bree gasping for breath beneath her.

"Oh, God…Logan!" Bree trembled, her hips suspended off the hardwood, her nipples like hardened jewels against Logan's chest, and insides clenching around Logan's fingers.

Logan pulled back, wanting to watch Bree fall into the tranquil moment of her orgasm, and found Bree watching her, wanting her, loving her, and everything felt so right—this moment, the next moment, all the following moments, were already perfect.

Logan drove harder, faster, fucking her, hard, delving her fingers palm-deep, reaching the very depths of Bree. Her own legs trembled, her open jeans loose around her hips, her back muscles tight, but she kept on fucking her, driving her closer, ignoring the biting grip of cramps.

Bree's lips parted, her eyes still tagged on Logan, and

then her back arched and she dug her head against the floor. "Oh, fuck…Logan, I'm coming!"

Her insides sucked Logan deeper, gripping her fingers in tight pulses. She cried out, grabbing for Logan.

Logan lowered herself over Bree and then her own orgasm exploded through her body, through her mind, sucking her soul down with every spasm.

She was vaguely aware of Bree saying her name over and over, holding her, pumping against her, around her fingers. It was the most tear-jerking experience of her life. She felt drained from the emotions alone.

When Logan tried to pull away to look at her once again, Bree tightened her hold, and rocked beneath her, sucking in healthy gulps of air, her insides trembling with renewed pumps.

Logan kept pumping inside her until she felt the energy drain from them both, then fell in a boneless heap over her, fingers still buried inside her lightly pulsing depths.

"That was incredible." Bree gently stroked Logan's back and her shoulder.

Logan rolled onto her side and nuzzled her face into Bree's neck then pressed a kiss against her flesh, sated and relaxed. "There's more, sexy. I'm not done with you yet."

Bree chuckled and laid her head against Logan's chest. Logan smoothed her hair down and pulled her closer. There was no getting close enough to Bree. God, those arms felt right, like she'd been meant for them, meant for each other.

Logan stared into those tranquil, satisfied eyes, love filling her heart. "Did your wish come true?"

Bree kissed the tip of her nose. "It's getting there." She leaned down and captured Logan's lips then curled her tongue inside.

Once again, Logan's world rocked and spun. As frightening as the sensation was, it was incredibly calming.

Bree hummed and pulled back as her legs tightened around Logan's waist. She circled her hips as she nipped Logan's earlobe, then whispered, "I've got some wicked exploration of my to do now. Then my wish will be complete." She shoved Logan onto her back.

Logan smiled, very much liking the feel of Bree wanting more, her brash control. But first, she had some unfinished business to tend to—the real reason she'd come to Bree's tonight.

She unclamped Bree's lean legs from her waist and picked up the book still lying against the front door. "You never looked at this."

Bree sat up and brushed long blond locks from her face. She studied the book for a second before she took the bound pages. "What is it?"

"Open it." Logan sat beside her and kissed her shoulder. "It's yours."

Bree opened the cover and a smile broke out across her face as she read the dedication on the flyleaf… *To B, the very special lady whose words turned this project from a dream, to reality. I can't thank you enough.*

Logan watched her expression, watched her chew the inside of her cheek, with a smile quivering her lips. The look was more earth shattering than watching the first photo shuttle down the chute. There was pride in those eyes, all for Logan, for her accomplishments.

Bree trailed her fingers along the bottom edge of the photo. "This is…precious, and priceless. It's beautiful."

Logan stared down at the book, watched Bree turn another page. "It's the only printed version until release date and I wanted you to have it. I couldn't wait another six months to show you that you were right." She raised her hand and turned Bree's face around. "It's not nearly as beautiful as you." She almost cringed with her words, having not said them to too many women in her life, hell, if any. Those words gave away power, but for some reason, she didn't feel any less powerful after having said them to Bree. Actually, just the opposite. She felt like queen of the world, like saying the words gave her infinite power over her own fate.

Every word was the truth, along with all the other sweet-nothings she wanted to tell Bree—how her hair was so soft, how it smelled of sweet fruit, how she wanted to wake up beside her tomorrow, and the next, and any other morning she'd allow Logan, how she wanted to hold her hand and walk barefoot in the park, how she wanted to feed her strawberries and champagne in the bath or ice cream in bed, and then cuddle with her over some sappy chick flick.

God, what was she thinking? How could she want those things, and with a person as intellectual as Bree Hendricks?

Bree cocked her head. "I can't believe you did this for me, because of what I said?"

Logan considered her question. Had she? Hadn't she? She slowly nodded. "Yes, I did it for you. I had to…I've been doing way too many things for my own selfish needs. Doing this for you showed me what a disgrace I've been."

Bree lowered her lashes. "I'm sorry. I should have never said that…it was unfair."

Logan hooked her finger under Bree's chin. "You're wrong. What you said, it opened my eyes." She kissed Bree's cheek. "I can't thank you enough."

Bree looked away. "I went to your apartment tonight… you opened the magazine again. I'm thrilled."

Logan perked up at the confession. "Really? You went to my apartment?" She relished the words, thankful she hadn't been home. Nothing could have been as sweet as this particular surprise visit. "What were you looking for there?"

"You."

Logan took the book from her hands and dropped it onto the floor. Just hearing that Bree had come looking for her, that she'd wanted her, God, it gave her renewed hope they might have some future after this night of passion ended.

She pushed Bree onto her back and kneed her legs apart, towering over her, owning her. "And what exactly were you looking for, besides me?"

Bree licked her lips. "Satisfaction."

"Ahhh." Logan rolled her hips against Bree's pussy. "That's right. I forgot. Seems the matchmaker is *unmatched*." She jarred her hips against Bree and she cried out.

Bree pushed off the floor, her legs hooked over Logan's thighs, then pressed her hand flat against Logan's chest and shoved her backward until Logan uncurled her legs and flattened out. Bree straddled her hips. "Yes, thanks to you, I'm sexually deprived. I should have just fucked you in your apartment, and in the car, and on the car, and in the restaurant, in that fucking coat closet, instead of trying not to cheat on a relationship that had run its course long before we ever met."

Logan grinned and palmed Bree's hips, pushing upward, circling, her body yearning for satisfaction. "Tsk tsk. Can't have the pleasure planner in that type of predicament, now can we." She gently tugged Bree's hair until she was flat against her chest, then whispered against her throat. "What more can I do to *relieve* your frustrations?"

Bree leaned toward Logan and placed her index finger against her lips. "Just lie still and let me show you. Believe me, you'll enjoy it." She wiggled her way down Logan's body, taking her jeans and briefs with her. She tugged them off Logan's legs and tossed them to the side.

With a wicked smile, she crawled between Logan's legs and forcefully wedged them apart.

Logan's stomach churned, love, and lust, and everything else powerful enough to find a way inside her emotions, rammed into her all at once, along with Bree's fingers. She sucked in a healthy breath and fisted her hands, gripping and relaxing, wanting Bree in her arms when she came again, this time by Bree's hands.

For some reason, Logan knew and accepted Bree wanted her like this, at her mercy, with Bree completely in control. She drove her fingers deep, deeper still, then flicked her tongue along her clit, dragging it dangerously slowly across her hood before she lowered her face and started all over again.

Logan was coming undone, so close to coming, so close to falling into the dark abyss, somewhere she'd never been before. She briefly wondered if she'd leave this night the same woman, prayed she wouldn't.

A look of smug satisfaction masked Bree's face as she drove those pleasing fingers deep inside her, thrusting hard against her pleasure spot, then backing out slowly, driving in once again, all while her tongue lapped at Logan like a cat.

Exquisite heat curled in her belly, cramping her insides into a tight knot, and then she shattered, screaming out her relief as the world dissolved into an unimaginable kaleidoscope of rainbow lights and sweet music.

Bree reared over her body and fell on top of her, her hand still buried deep inside Logan's pussy, and Logan, still flying apart, grasping and pawing at her, clinging with a death grip around Bree's back, pumping against her hand.

Hot tears stung her eyes. What in God's name for? Had

Bree emotionally jerked her to tears—real, caring tears with only an orgasm? She'd heard about such things happening, had even driven a few of her own lovers to those sweet tears, but never, ever, had she encountered them herself.

When her body went limp, with Bree's fingers still wiggling inside her, Logan opened her eyes and stared up at her—at the most breathtaking woman she'd ever had the pleasure of meeting, of knowing, of kissing, and now making love to.

The pleasure planner was in her arms, and she wanted to be here, and from the look of those soft eyes, she didn't want to leave.

When her insides ceased pumping, she pushed a lone lock of curl back from Bree's face and kissed her lips. "Incredible."

Bree smiled and kissed her. Her fingers splayed under the crook of Logan's jaw. Her other hand joined the first until her palms were around Logan's cheeks, keeping her in place. "God only knows how, or why, but I want more from you, Logan Delaney. Tonight, tomorrow…but I won't beg you, and I won't chase you. I won't give you any part of my heart until you've earned it."

Logan was shocked. Had Bree just confessed love, or a future? Was that too much to ask? The thought was too much to bear, and those eyes were lying. There was already love there, and God help her, she was going to earn every ounce of it.

She stared up into those breathtaking eyes, so full of want, packed with too much emotion. Logan loved her. She didn't know where or when it'd happened, but she did. She loved this woman, and she prayed somehow, Bree would eventually trust her.

With a smile, she pressed her lips against Bree's. "Then I'll chase you forever."

About the Author

Larkin Rose lives in a "blink and you've missed it" town in the beautiful state of South Carolina with her partner, a portion of their seven brats, and two chunky grandsons. Her writing career began four years ago when the voices in her head wouldn't stop their constant chatter. After ruling out multiple personalities, and hitting the keyboard, a writer was born.

Her short works appear in *Ultimate Lesbian Erotica 2008* and *Wetter 2008* (both writing as Sheri Livingston).

The voices continue. The clatter of keys continues. The birth of erotic creations carries on.

Books Available From Bold Strokes Books

The Pleasure Planner by Larkin Rose. Pleasure purveyor Bree Hendricks treats love like a commodity until Logan Delaney makes Bree the client in her own game. (978-1-60282-121-7)

everafter by Nell Stark and Trinity Tam. Valentine Darrow is bitten by a vampire on her way to propose to her lover Alexa Newland, and their lives and love are placed in mortal jeopardy. (978-1-60282-119-4)

Summer Winds by Andrews & Austin. When Maggie Turner hires a ranch hand to help work her thousand acres, she never expects to be attracted to the very young, very female Cash Tate. (978-1-60282-120-0)

Beggar of Love by Lee Lynch. Jefferson is the lover every woman wants to be—or to have. A revealing saga of lesbian sexuality. (978-1-60282-122-4)

The Seduction of Moxie by Colette Moody. When 1930s Broadway actress Violet London meets speakeasy singer Moxie Valette, she is instantly attracted and her Hollywood trip takes an unexpected turn. (978-1-60282-114-9)

Goldenseal by Gill McKnight. When Amy Fortune returns to her childhood home, she discovers something sinister in the air—but is former lover Leone Garoul stalking her or protecting her? (978-1-60282-115-6)

Romantic Interludes 2: Secrets edited by Radclyffe and Stacia Seaman. An anthology of sensual lesbian love stories: passion, surprises, and secret desires. (978-1-60282-116-3)

Femme Noir by Clara Nipper. Nora Delaney meets her match in Max Abbott, a sex-crazed dame who may or may not have the information Nora needs to solve a murder—but can she contain her lust for Max long enough to find out? (978-1-60282-117-0)

The Reluctant Daughter by Lesléa Newman. Heartwarming, heartbreaking, and ultimately triumphant—the story every daughter recognizes of the lifelong struggle for our mothers to really see us. (978-1-60282-118-7)

Erosistible by Gill McKnight. When Win Martin arrives at a luxurious Greek hotel for a much-anticipated week of sun and sex with her new girlfriend, she is stunned to find her ex-girlfriend, Benny, is the proprietor. Aeros Ebook. (978-1-60282-134-7)

Looking Glass Lives by Felice Picano. Cousins Roger and Alistair become lifelong friends and discover their sexuality amidst the backdrop of twentieth-century gay culture. (978-1-60282-089-0)

Breaking the Ice by Kim Baldwin. Nothing is easy about life above the Arctic Circle—except, perhaps, falling in love. At least that's what pilot Bryson Faulkner hopes when she meets Karla Edwards. (978-1-60282-087-6)

It Should Be a Crime by Carsen Taite. Two women fulfill their mutual desire with a night of passion, neither expecting more until law professor Morgan Bradley and student Parker Casey meet again…in the classroom. (978-1-60282-086-9)

Rough Trade edited by Todd Gregory. Top male erotica writers pen their own hot, sexy versions of the term "rough trade," producing some of the hottest, nastiest, and most dangerous fiction ever published. (978-1-60282-092-0)

The High Priest and the Idol by Jane Fletcher. Jemeryl and Tevi's relationship is put to the test when the Guardian sends Jemeryl on a mission that puts her not only in harm's way, but back into the sights of a previous lover. (978-1-60282-085-2)

Point of Ignition by Erin Dutton. Amid a blaze that threatens to consume them both, firefighter Kate Chambers and property owner Alexi Clark redefine love and trust. (978-1-60282-084-5)

Secrets in the Stone by Radclyffe. Reclusive sculptor Rooke Tyler suddenly finds herself the object of two very different women's affections, and choosing between them will change her life forever. (978-1-60282-083-8)

Dark Garden by Jennifer Fulton. Vienna Blake and Mason Cavender are sworn enemies—who can't resist each other. Something has to give. (978-1-60282-036-4)

Late in the Season by Felice Picano. Set on Fire Island, this is the story of an unlikely pair of friends—a gay composer in his late thirties and an eighteen-year-old schoolgirl. (978-1-60282-082-1)

Punishment with Kisses by Diane Anderson-Minshall. Will Megan find the answers she seeks about her sister Ashley's murder or will her growing relationship with one of Ash's exes blind her to the real truth? (978-1-60282-081-4)

September Canvas by Gun Brooke. When Deanna Moore meets TV personality Faythe she is reluctantly attracted to her, but will Faythe side with the people spreading rumors about Deanna? (978-1-60282-080-7)

No Leavin' Love by Larkin Rose. Beautiful, successful Mercedes Miller thinks she can resume her affair with ranch foreman Sydney Campbell, but the rules have changed. (978-1-60282-079-1)

Between the Lines by Bobbi Marolt. When romance writer Gail Prescott meets actress Tannen Albright, she develops feelings that she usually only experiences through her characters. (978-1-60282-078-4)

Blue Skies by Ali Vali. Commander Berkley Levine leads an elite group of pilots on missions ordered by her ex-lover Captain Aidan Sullivan and everything is on the line—including love. (978-1-60282-077-7)

The Lure by Felice Picano. When Noel Cummings is recruited by the police to go undercover to find a killer, his life will never be the same. (978-1-60282-076-0)

Death of a Dying Man by J.M. Redmann. Mickey Knight, Private Eye and partner of Dr. Cordelia James, doesn't need a drop-dead gorgeous assistant—not until nature steps in. (978-1-60282-075-3)

Justice for All by Radclyffe. Dell Mitchell goes undercover to expose a human traffic ring and ends up in the middle of an even deadlier conspiracy. (978-1-60282-074-6)

Sanctuary by I. Beacham. Cate Canton faces one major obstacle to her goal of crushing her business rival, Dita Newton—her uncontrollable attraction to Dita. (978-1-60282-055-5)

The Sublime and Spirited Voyage of Original Sin by Colette Moody. Pirate Gayle Malvern finds the presence of an abducted seamstress, Celia Pierce, a welcome distraction until the captive comes to mean more to her than is wise. (978-1-60282-054-8)

Suspect Passions by VK Powell. Can two women, a city attorney and a beat cop, put aside their differences long enough to see that they're perfect for each other? (978-1-60282-053-1)

Just Business by Julie Cannon. Two women who come together—each for her own selfish needs—discover that love can never be as simple as a business transaction. (978-1-60282-052-4)

Sistine Heresy by Justine Saracen. Adrianna Borgia, survivor of the Borgia court, presents Michelangelo with the greatest temptations of his life while struggling with soul-threatening desires for the painter Raphaela. (978-1-60282-051-7)

Radical Encounters by Radclyffe. An out-of-bounds, outside-the-lines collection of provocative, superheated erotica by award-winning romance and erotica author Radclyffe. (978-1-60282-050-0)

Thief of Always by Kim Baldwin & Xenia Alexiou. Stealing a diamond to save the world should be easy for Elite Operative Mishael Taylor, but she didn't figure on love getting in the way. (978-1-60282-049-4)

X by JD Glass. When X-hacker Charlie Riven is framed for a crime she didn't commit, she accepts help from an unlikely source—sexy Treasury Agent Elaine Harper. (978-1-60282-048-7)

The Middle of Somewhere by Clifford Henderson. Eadie T. Pratt sets out on a road trip in search of a new life and ends up in the middle of somewhere she never expected. (978-1-60282-047-0)

Paybacks by Gabrielle Goldsby. Cameron Howard wants to avoid her old nemesis Mackenzie Brandt but their high school reunion brings up more than just memories. (978-1-60282-046-3)

Uncross My Heart by Andrews & Austin. When a radio talk show diva sets out to interview a female priest, the two women end up at odds and neither heaven nor earth is safe from their feelings. (978-1-60282-045-6)

Fireside by Cate Culpepper. Mac, a therapist, and Abby, a nurse, fall in love against the backdrop of friendship, healing, and defending one's own within the Fireside shelter. (978-1-60282-044-9)

A Pirate's Heart by Catherine Friend. When rare book librarian Emma Boyd searches for a long-lost treasure map, she learns the hard way that pirates still exist in today's world—some modern pirates steal maps, others steal hearts. (978-1-60282-040-1)

Trails Merge by Rachel Spangler. Parker Riley escapes the high-powered world of politics to Campbell Carson's ski resort—and their mutual attraction produces anything but smooth running. (978-1-60282-039-5)

Dreams of Bali by C.J. Harte. Madison Barnes worships work, power, and success, and she's never allowed anyone to interfere—that is, until she runs into Karlie Henderson Stockard. Aeros EBook (978-1-60282-070-8)

The Limits of Justice by John Morgan Wilson. Benjamin Justice and reporter Alexandra Templeton search for a killer in a mysterious compound in the remote California desert. (978-1-60282-060-9)

Designed for Love by Erin Dutton. Jillian Sealy and Wil Johnson don't much like each other, but they do have to work together—and what they desire most is not what either of them had planned. (978-1-60282-038-8)

Calling the Dead by Ali Vali. Six months after Hurricane Katrina, NOLA Detective Sept Savoie is a cop who thinks making a relationship work is harder than catching a serial killer—but her current case may prove her wrong. (978-1-60282-037-1)

Shots Fired by MJ Williamz. Kyla and Echo seem to have the perfect relationship and the perfect life until someone shoots at Kyla—and Echo is the most likely suspect. (978-1-60282-035-7)

truelesbianlove.com by Carsen Taite. Mackenzie Lewis and Dr. Jordan Wagner have very different ideas about love, but they discover that truelesbianlove is closer than a click away. Aeros EBook (978-1-60282-069-2)

Justice at Risk by John Morgan Wilson. Benjamin Justice's blind date leads to a rare opportunity for legitimate work, but a reckless risk changes his life forever. (978-1-60282-059-3)

Run to Me by Lisa Girolami. Burned by the four-letter word called love, the only thing Beth Standish wants to do is run for—or maybe from—her life. (978-1-60282-034-0)

Split the Aces by Jove Belle. In the neon glare of Sin City, two women ride a wave of passion that threatens to consume them in a world of fast money and fast times. (978-1-60282-033-3)

Uncharted Passage by Julie Cannon. Two women on a vacation that turns deadly face down one of nature's most ruthless killers—and find themselves falling in love. (978-1-60282-032-6)

Night Call by Radclyffe. All medevac helicopter pilot Jett McNally wants to do is fly and forget about the horror and heartbreak she left behind in the Middle East, but anesthesiologist Tristan Holmes has other plans. (978-1-60282-031-9)

Lake Effect Snow by C.P. Rowlands. News correspondent Annie T. Booker and FBI Agent Sarah Moore struggle to stay one step ahead of disaster as Annie's life becomes the war zone she once reported on. Aeros EBook (978-1-60282-068-5)

I Dare You by Larkin Rose. Stripper by night, corporate raider by day, Kelsey's only looking for sex and power, until she meets a woman who stirs her heart and her body. (978-1-60282-030-2)

Truth Behind the Mask by Lesley Davis. Erith Baylor is drawn to Sentinel Pagan Osborne's quiet strength, but the secrets between them strain duty and family ties. (978-1-60282-029-6)

Cooper's Deale by KI Thompson. Two would-be lovers and a decidedly inopportune murder spell trouble for Addy Cooper, no matter which way the cards fall. (978-1-60282-028-9)

Romantic Interludes 1: Discovery ed. by Radclyffe and Stacia Seaman. An anthology of sensual, erotic contemporary love stories from the best-selling Bold Strokes authors. (978-1-60282-027-2)

Homecoming by Nell Stark. Sarah Storm loses everything that matters—family, future dreams, and love—will her new "straight" roommate cause Sarah to take a chance at happiness? (978-1-60282-024-1)